The Consuming

Book 4 in the Reign of the Lion Series

By

VJJ Dunn

HEA Publishers
PO Box 591
Douglas, AZ 85608-0591
Or email: author@vjjdunn.com

Table of Contents

Author's Note

Eschatology: The doctrine of the "last things."

Eschatology is a tricky thing to write about. The thousand-year-period following the Tribulation has been called the most argued theological supposition.

And it's just that — supposition.

While the Reign of the Lion Series is based on the Millennial Period, it is just fiction. Fantasy. An author's imagination.

So much time has been spent in the teaching of the Millennial Period (Revelation 20:1-6). But truly, no one can give a true account of what it's going to be like.

I always try to stay true to the teachings of the Bible and how I envision Abba (my Daddy), but again, the stories I write are but fiction. Please always turn to Scripture for any verification or clarification... or just because you need a refreshing.

This book is the end of the series and I hope you enjoyed it. What comes next? Better question, what happens after the millennial time? I don't think I have enough imagination to write about something THAT splendid.

Regardless of how amazing and awesome and beyond imagination Heaven and the New Earth after this millennial period will be, it's only going to be that way because HE will be there! And you too ☐

Blessings!

Prologue

THE UNIFORM was gorgeous, crafted from some mysterious silvery metal buffed to such a high sheen that it was difficult to look at in the sun, adorned with intricate golden designs representing the Trinity. Epaulets, bracers and poleyns, or knee guards, added a decorative touch, leading to very ornate armor.

As she ran a polishing cloth over one of the leg harnesses, Allie thought that she kind of loved it. But at the same time, she wasn't thrilled with the fact that it was a necessity that she wear it in the first place.

Especially not *where* she needed to wear it.

The invading army's camp, where those who'd chosen to side with the enemy were counting the days until they could attack. They were marching to fight against the Creator of the universe for His holy city.

They were hardhearted. Stubborn. Deceived.

Morons, Allie snorted to herself.

"I heard that, child." The chiding voice came from behind her and Allie laughed.

"Of course You did. You hear everything, even my less-than lovely thoughts," she said as He came around to stand in front of her. She lifted her eyes and sucked in a breath; no matter how many countless times she'd been in Abba's presence, He never failed to steal her air. He was quite literally *breathtaking.*

"Some of those thoughts should be left in my brain, You know," she smirked at Him.

Abba's glowing face crinkled. "You are absolutely correct about that," He said as He cocked a scolding eyebrow at her. The look was ruined when He winked.

Allie laughed as she felt her cheeks heat. She knew He was teasing her, but still... it was the truth. She'd never been good at corralling her thoughts.

It was definitely a good thing that Abba was so forgiving.

She set the piece she'd been working on aside and stood. Without invitation, she moved into Abba's always open arms. She wrapped her arms around Him and breathed in His amazing scent — it was the aroma of clouds, of rain in the air on a clear, cool evening.

No other smell could compare.

He ran a soothing hand along her spine and back up again. Allie sighed in pleasure, feeling better than she ever remembered feeling in that moment. Being comforted by the Creator was incomparable.

"Better?" He asked, His rich voice rumbling through her. The thunder to accompany the rain.

She nodded against Him and took that as her cue to step away from the embrace, much as she hated to. But she had been given her assignment and Abba had said there wasn't much time left before the army attacked, and she still needed to say goodbye to her family and friends.

Abba wasn't quite ready to release her, though. He held her by the shoulder with one of His hands and with the other, he tucked a wayward strand of hair behind her ear. He then slid His finger along her jaw.

"This is a very difficult assignment you've been given, daughter," He said and Allie didn't miss the way He grimaced slightly. She wondered exactly what it was He *wasn't* saying.

"You and Alejandro will be in the midst of those who hate Me, and by association, will hate you because of Me. They cannot stand what we stand for. But you're not there for them, remember that. You're only there for those who have been deceived, who believe they are fighting for the side of good. Your mission is to tell them otherwise."

Allie nodded and Abba placed both hands on her shoulders. He gave her a very slight shake.

"Don't forget that you must get in and get out as rapidly as possible. We don't want you being captured again." He gave her a crooked smile at that, which she returned with a smirk.

No, I definitely do NOT want that again.

The last two times she'd been captured were horrible. The first time, she'd hung in The Pit, in the very same place Lucifer had hung in chains for the Millennial Period. The second time, she'd been Lucifer's "honored guest," aka, unwilling captive, who he'd used to deceive so many, saying the Remnant Mistress had chosen to side with him.

Even though she'd been wined and dined while in Lucifer's clutches, she much preferred The Pit to being used like that.

Both sucked though.

"Remember too that it won't take long for Lucifer to discover that you're among his army and he wants more than anything else to recapture you. You humiliated him... high five," Abba grinned and held up His hand. Allie chuckled as she smacked it with hers.

"He wants revenge. If he captures you again, my sweet girl, I don't think he'll be nearly as accommodating as he was last time."

Allie shivered. If being held in shackles, unable to escape, being guarded by leering, pervy demons was "accommodating," then she really didn't want to know what Lucifer would be like if he wasn't playing the gracious host.

"And don't forget about the bounty that is still on your head," He continued. "There will be many wanting to capture you for that reason alone."

Abba gave her another small shake and leaned

forward, making sure she was focused on Him.

"Just do not get caught."

Chapter 1

I KNOW YOU do, but you can't," Allie moaned as she wiped her cheek. This was the third time Nick had asked, insisted and begged to go with her on her new assignment.

"You know, I think our vows said something about obeying," he said with a scowl as he crossed his arms angrily over his chest.

Allie's eyes rolled. "You're kidding me, right? Were you not there when Abba married us? He never said anything about anyone obeying, except that we're all supposed to obey Him! And that's what I'm doing, obeying *The Creator!*"

She shouted the last, then instantly felt bad when his face fell.

"I'm sorry," she said as she stepped up to her husband. He reluctantly uncrossed his arms and she stepped into them.

"It's just that I'm stressed, you know?" Allie murmured against his neck. "I mean, the last thing I want to do is leave you, leave the team, and go off on my own again." She sniffled.

"I don't exactly have a great track record when I go out on my own."

Nick's chest vibrated with laughter. "No," he agreed, "you don't." He sighed then and tightened his arms, then put his lips to her ear.

"I know you don't have a choice and it *is* an honorable mission. I'm... it's just that I'm upset on multiple levels here. First, you just got back from your holiday with Lucifer—" he fake-grimaced when Allie punched him in the ribs.

There was laughter in his voice when he continued. "I was so worried about you when you were gone, even though Abba kept reassuring me that you were fine. Finally, I get you back, and now you're going right back there." Another heavy sigh lifted his chest.

"Just promise me you'll be extra careful this time, okay?" he murmured as his arms tightened around her once more.

In the past, Allie would have made light of the subject, joking that she could take on the entire enemy army on her own. She certainly knew better now. After being captured so easily twice now, humility was her newly acquired trait.

"I promise. Abba warned me to watch my back. We'll transfer out of any situation that turns bad. I'm not gung-ho for a fight anymore, so I won't hang around to bait the masses," she smirked.

She was the new and improved Alessandra.

Nick kissed her then, a silent promise of devotion and adoration between the wedded, before stepping back and abruptly leaving the apartment without a backward glance.

Allie watched him go with a heavy heart, then

turned to look at her surroundings. She was going to miss her apartment, especially her cloud-like bed. Despite her pleading, Abba had insisted that she and Alejandro not transfer back to the Remnant quarters each day, but instead, rely on the hospitality of others, as the original disciples had done when they'd gone out to witness to the masses.

She just wasn't sure how the Mistress of the Remnant Warriors and the Chief Witness to Those Born During the New Age were going to be received. Probably not happily.

Allie wished that Charo had returned from her mission. It had been over a month since Allie had asked her bobcat friend to check on Serariel, the angel who'd sacrificed himself to save Allie... and who now hung in The Pit. The idea of him being there, alone, filled Allie with such sadness that she tried very hard not to think about it.

Some of the angels had become very dear to her.

Like Zad and Metatron, who sat on the couch watching her. She sighed and moved to sit on the coffee table, facing them. The angels didn't look any happier with her mission than Nick had been.

Allie reached out and took each of their hands in one of her own. The angels were so large that they didn't even have to lean forward. She stared at her small hands being swallowed by their massive ones.

No one said anything. There really weren't any words left to be said. The angels were just as upset with her new assignment as Nick was. Not that she

9

was any happier with it. The only one happy with the whole thing was Alejandro.

For some reason, though, Allie felt like this was the last time she'd see her family, at least in her current body. And in the next life, everything was going to be so different, even the relationships they had with one another.

Metatron gently squeezed her fingers while Zad ran his thumb over the back of her hand. Allie looked up. Both angels were staring at their joined hands.

"Gonna miss you guys," she whispered. Anything louder and she knew her voice would crack.

Zad's throat worked and Allie wondered if angels could cry. She'd never seen them shed actual tears, but she had seen an awful lot of different emotions crossing their faces in the time she'd known them. A lot of the time, it was annoyance... especially from Metatron.

Now, both her best friends looked miserable. That was the last thing she wanted.

"I'll visit you in spirit," she told them. "Probably bug the crap out of you. I'll be like the annoying little sister you can't escape." She grinned, while Zad smirked.

"And that'll be different... how?" Zad joked. Allie stuck her tongue out at him and he grinned.

Metatron's expression didn't change. He didn't look up either. Allie sighed, released their hands and moved to sit on the huge angel's lap. The action surprised him, and he scowled at her, but Allie could tell he was pleased by her affection. Especially when his arms wrapped around her.

Allie knew others wondered if her relationship with the two angels was too intimate. She didn't care what they thought. There was obviously nothing sexual going on. First and foremost, that would be a grievous sin and one that Abba absolutely would have punished. But second, she loved Zad and Metatron like brothers and she knew they felt the same. She really was the little sister, who could sometimes be annoying.

Okay, maybe most times.

Allie wrapped her arms around Metatron's neck and leaned forward to press her forehead to his. He closed his eyes and sucked in a stuttering breath. She did the same.

"I'll be okay, big guy. Even if... the worst happens, it's just a short time until Judgement Day and then we move on to the next life. Easy peasy."

Metatron's shoulders shook slightly. He didn't laugh often and in fact, rarely smiled, but when he did either, it was usually because of something Allie said.

She kissed his cheek, then leaned over and grabbed Zad by the front of his tunic and pulled him toward her. She pecked his cheek too, then patted it and pushed herself up.

"Well, time to get going," she sighed. "I'll see you guys around." *Probably not.* The angels looked like their thoughts were mirroring her own.

With a growl, Metatron jumped to his feet so fast that Allie started to fall back over the table. Before she could even right herself, he snatched her up and clutched her to his chest. It was much like Nick had done, except with Nick her feet weren't dangling two feet off the floor. Instinctually, she wrapped her hands around the angel's neck.

"Do not underestimate Lucifer, little warrior," he murmured quietly in her ear. "His deceptions are unfathomable. You have only seen his very best side. He is capable of so much worse."

Allie wondered why he felt the need to keep his words quiet. Zad could hear a butterfly fart in the gardens three stories below with his super angel hearing, so she knew Metatron wasn't trying to keep anything from him. She wondered if it was because some of the demons had that danged invisibility power and he knew one of them was lurking about her apartment.

"If you need help, transfer to us if you can; if not, visit us in the spirit. Zadkiel and I will keep our senses open for your presence at all times. If need us, we will be there, even at the risk of disobeying Abba. We will not have a repeat of the past."

Allie nodded slightly. "I will," she assured him, then kissed his cheek again before he set her back down. After one more hug from Zad, she walked out the door and on to her next adventure.

Unfortunately, this adventure sounded more like a suicide mission.

Chapter 2

THE FIRST STOP they made was at a small village not far from the Remnant quarters. Allie was surprised; she had thought that the Remnant's new place was farther away from civilization.

And it made her realize that she needed to pay a lot more attention.

Abba had given them a map to follow. He told Allie and Alejandro that they "would not be welcome in all places," but they were to share the truth everywhere they went and move on if the truth was rejected.

More than anything, Allie hated the thought of that. She couldn't stand being somewhere where she knew she wasn't wanted.

It was a warm day, so they had the top retracted, which made the trip a bit more tolerable. Allie had always liked the feel of the wind in her face, although she would have preferred to transfer from place to place. But for whatever reason, Abba wanted them to travel via contrans, which was her second favorite mode of travel. The hovercraft made her feel like a Skywalker.

"We just need lightsabers," she yelled to Alejandro. He cocked his head at her in confusion. Allie laughed; she was used to that look. Very few in the New Age understood her Old Age references.

Alejandro was practically bouncing in his seat. His mission over the past millennium had been to witness to those who'd been born after the Tribulation, but he'd never been able to do so on such a large scale as Lucifer's army.

To say he was excited was putting it mildly.

His exuberance made Allie smile. Witnessing to the lost and leading them to Abba was something that made her friend's face glow. Even when he was a child during the Tribulation, he would crawl up on top of anything that would put him above a crowd so they could see him and he then he would proceed to yell at the lost, basically threaten them.

At first it was funny, and Allie and the other adults would try to calm the child down, to hush him. But when hundreds and then thousands started coming to the Lord thanks to Alejandro's testimony, the adults started looking for places where the child could plant his feet and testify.

Allie parked the contrans well outside of the village because she didn't want to freak anyone out and send them running. Usually, when a contrans appeared, it was for the purpose of hauling off a Judas — aka, a sinner — and villagers tended to avoid them.

Alejandro practically leapt out of the sleek transport and Allie knew he was planning on barging into the village and start yelling at them about how wonderful Abba was. She knew that wasn't going to be the best plan, so she called out.

"Andro, wait. We need to assess each situation before we go charging in, Custer."

He cocked his head at her. "Custer?"

Allie waved her hand. "Never mind. He was a general — uh, like a military leader — from the Old Age. Made a bad decision and charged into a battle and got himself and a bunch of his men killed."

Alejandro's eyes widened. "Oh."

She didn't want to throw a wet blanket on the guy, though. She moved around the contrans and laid her hand on Alejandro's shoulder.

"I just want to make sure that you get to witness to as many people as possible. We don't want to get dead before you tell the very last soul to be saved about Abba's salvation, right?"

He laughed and nodded. Allie squeezed her old friend's shoulder "So, same as before when I took you into the cities during the Gathering. Keep an eye out for any attacks and especially watch for demons. Stick with me at all times, within arm's reach so that I can transfer us out of there if it comes to it. If any of the people do want salvation, then we round them up and direct them to The City."

Alejandro nodded in agreement and Allie turned to push the button to raise the top on the contrans and they turned to head toward the village.

"Look," Allie said as they walked through the village gate, pointing to what looked like the village's well. In her experience that was usually the center of a community and just like in the "old days" was where most of the people tended to congregate.

"Let's head over there."

The village was small, just a few dozen homes as far as Allie could tell. She doubted there was more than a hundred people living there. It didn't matter; even though Alejandro's mission for the past thousand years had been to reach as many as possible, even only one was one more child for Abba.

Over the millennium, Alejandro had witnessed to all the large metropolises, the cities and towns. He hadn't had much success so far, but Allie figured that now that Lucifer had been released and was gathering a huge army, people might realize that the "end was near."

Because it seriously was.

They passed a building and the sun's rays caught on Allie's uniform, sending beams of light in every direction. She felt like one of those balls in the Old Age, the ones that used to hang from the ceiling in the places people would go to dance.

She'd questioned Abba about His choice for her uniform. Before, she had a pretty plain black uniform that had just a bit of gold embellishment to distinguish her as a leader. But now — it was super flashy and painful to look at in the daylight. Abba had told her that the brightness of the uniform, along with the matching shield and sword, would draw people to her.

Judging by the villagers that were starting to come out of their homes, gawking, He was right. Allie felt like a clown in the circus.

She knew Alejandro would want to get above the crowd so he could be seen, so she ignored the oglers and led her friend to the well. Alejandro wasted no time, climbing up on the well's wall and facing the growing crowd.

Allie stood just to his side, on the ground, scanning the crowd, most of whom were women. It stood to reason that most of the men had joined Lucifer's army.

She reached out with all her senses as Metatron had taught her. She didn't want to move into the spirit, though, because she had a tendency to get somewhat... enamored, by the spiritual surroundings. Metatron said that in the spirit she was like a ferret enthralled with a shiny object.

The crowd seemed interested in what they were doing, which was no big shock. Allie couldn't sense any malevolence, though, relief filling her. She'd hate to have to stab someone before breakfast.

Kidding, Abba! Just kidding. Allie could swear she heard Him snort.

"Friends," Alejandro shouted just above her right shoulder, making Allie jump. Some of the villagers noticed and snickered. Her cheeks grew hot then. *Some big, bad Remnant I am...*

"We have come here today to tell you some very

good news!" Alejandro yelled. Allie wanted to pinch his calf to get his attention and tell him he didn't need to yell; everyone in the village apparently was already surrounding them and it amounted to maybe one hundred people. But Alejandro usually operated at full volume.

Allie had to admit, his announcement made them pay attention. They were probably hoping to hear that they were going to get some sort of special treatment or something. Which, if they accepted Alejandro's message, they definitely would.

For all eternity.

"Did you know that there is a plan for you?" Alejandro asked. "That in a short time, you will be entering into a new time, one that will last for all of eternity?" A few people looked confused and some skeptical.

"It's true," he yelled again. "Soon, very soon, we all will be spending the rest of all of time in one of two places — heaven or hell. You may not have heard that Abba, the Creator God, wants you to be with Him, in heaven, for the rest of eternity. He loves you, all of you. You are His creation. You breathe because His breath has filled your lungs. You walk because He gave you the ability to do so. You see, hear, smell, taste, feel, because He designed you to be able to do so.

"While He wants *all* of His creation to be with Him, He also wants it to be your choice. He does not, and will not, force anyone to make the decision to be with Him. He wants His unconditional love returned to Him from His children because they *want* to love Him, because they just can't help but love Him, and not because they feel obligated to.

"This is why you have a choice now, a choice of where you'll spend all of time after this period ends. You see, with Abba life will be beautiful. So amazingly beautiful that it cannot even be described with mere words. There, you will love, you will be loved, you will *become* love. Nothing you have ever experienced here will compare to the wonderment of that life."

Allie noticed that some people seemed interested in what Alejandro was saying, while others seemed a bit bored, or maybe disappointed, that they weren't there to give them a handout.

Alejandro took a deep breath, like he was getting ready to impart dreaded news. Which he was.

"The alternative to an incredibly wondrous life with Abba is to cast your lot with Lucifer." He paused and Allie could see from the corner of her eye that he was looking at each person.

"What I just described in an eternity with Abba? You get the opposite with Lucifer. Side with him and you will be cast into outer darkness. *Outer darkness.* Do you know what this means? It means complete and total black. No light.

"Abba is light," Alejandro yelled. "Abba creates all light. When He is absent, light does not exist. No matter how bleak any darkness you may have encountered was, whether it be from lack of a moon, or inside a darkened room, you have never been in darkness such as this. Our human minds cannot fathom how horrifying it will be.

"But that isn't even the worst of it. Abba said there would be 'wailing and gnashing of teeth'. Why? Is it because of pain? Yes, but not physical pain. The pain will be far worse than the most excruciating agony you've ever experienced. Incomprehensible pain. Again... why? Because you will know that you made the wrong choice, that you chose to side with Lucifer and turn your back on Abba. You will know for all eternity that because of the wrong decision, you have no hope, no love, no light, no *nothing*. Your existence will be a miserable testament to the fact that you were deceived."

Alejandro started pacing then and Allie turned so she would be able to grab him in case his foot slipped off the rock wall of the well.

"Over the past few months, the world has been deceived. People have been led to believe that they are being healed by the very being who made them ill in the first place. They've been told that diseases, ailments and even poisonings have been cured by the only one who has the power to do so."

He stopped his pacing then and faced the crowd once more. "Do you know that Lucifer only has the power to heal such things because he is the one who *created* the problems in the first place?" He was practically screaming and Allie flinched again.

The guy was definitely on fire.

"Lucifer is the great deceiver. The ultimate liar!" Alejandro's voice rose to an even greater volume at the last part.

Allie sensed the shift in the crowd before any words were spoken. Her hand twitched, ready to draw her sword if need be.

"*You're* the liar!" a man shouted. "Lucifer came to our village and healed our people of a sickness that made us all like dead men walking around! If it weren't for him, we *would* have died!"

"You don't know what you're talking about!" another woman yelled. "Lucifer has done nothing but help us. He's given us food, medicine and has performed many miracles! What has Abba done for us? Nothing!"

She spit out Abba's name with such abhorrence that Allie's hand itched to take the lady's head from her shoulders.

No one talked about her Daddy that way.

But then she remembered Abba had warned her of this very thing. And had told her not to react. The fact that they would, or even *could,* hate Him was beyond her comprehension. Allie tried to think back to the time in the Old Age when she hadn't been one of His kids. She couldn't even remember it.

She shook off her anger. But just barely. The lady would keep her head... for a little longer at least.

The crowd was being fueled by the few who spoke up and Allie could see that this was one of those "shake the dust from your sandals" types of places. Alejandro was still making a valiant effort to reach them, to crack their hard hearts with truth's hammer, but it wasn't working.

When the angry group started edging closer, Allie knew they needed to get out of there. She reached up and tugged on Alejandro's robe, hard enough to bring him off the wall. He stumbled as he landed and she grabbed his shoulder, transferring them back to the contrans.

"Get in," she ordered her friend as she climbed in the driver's seat. Alejandro looked like he wanted to argue, wanted to go back into the midst of the mob and continue trying to reach them. When he took a step in that direction, Allie let out a growl.

"Andro," she said, warning in her voice. "Don't try it. I'd hate to have to transfer you back to Abba and tell Him you're not behaving."

She was teasing, but she also had no qualms about doing so. Her main job was to keep the Chief Witness safe. He had a job to do and she'd be darned if she'd lose him before he finished it.

Alejandro sighed, his shoulders slumping in defeat. He hiked his robe up and climbed into the contrans, then pulled the robe back down over his legs. Allie waited until he was settled, thinking how glad she was that she didn't have to wear the robes that many of Abba's elect wore. While her new uniform was a bit more cumbersome than her past uniforms had been, it was still a lot easier to move around in than what Alejandro was wearing.

'Course, he doesn't need to move around to yell at heathens, she thought, lips twitching.

As she maneuvered the contrans away from the village, Alejandro asked, "What's so funny?"

Allie shook her head. "Just thinking we're probably going to end up sleeping in the contrans if things keep going like that." It wasn't the only thing she'd been thinking, but she didn't think Alejandro would appreciate the fact that she'd been silently laughing at him.

"Yeah, you're probably right," he said quietly. "That didn't go at all like I'd hoped." He sounded so dejected that Allie felt bad for the guy.

She reached over and nabbed his hand. "Hey, don't take that personally. Abba did warn us that most wouldn't hear the truth. And you never know who *did* listen back there. It might not have been everyone, but I'm sure at least some of those people accepted what you had to say."

She wasn't really sure if she totally believed that, but they could hope at least.

Alejandro didn't reply to that, but he sighed heavily. "We need to make a better plan for the next place. I think I need to be more passionate."

Allie couldn't help the burst of laughter that escaped her. He turned and cocked an eyebrow at her. "What?"

She snickered. "Dude, if you get any more *passionate*, you're going to run everyone off, thinking you're about to explode."

Alejandro's mouth turned up at the corners, but he still looked dejected. Allie sighed then as she turned toward the west, heading for Mandeville, the next town according to Abba's map. Even though she'd been around for all of the millennium, she had only traveled to the cities and towns where Judas' resided so that she could hand out the punishment they'd earned for whatever sin they committed.

"Maybe just focus on Abba and not Lucifer," Allie suggested. "The jerk has had a long time now to deceive these people, so they have him up on a pedestal. Try focusing on Abba's good instead."

Alejandro nodded. "I just hate the idea that those people—" he gestured back toward the village fading from sight behind them, "—are going to spend eternity in hell."

Allie sighed. "Yeah, I know. I felt like that when I was traveling with the army. A sea of faces, too many to count, and every single one of them was lost. It was… heartbreaking." Her voice was barely above a whisper.

She sighed then, heavily. "It's hard. Abba's heart breaks over it too." Allie reached over and patted Alejandro's hand.

"We can only do the best we can with what we're

given. You were given the blessing of evangelism and we're doing the best we can to let you use that gift. What the people do with that gift, with the truth you give them, is up to them. Remember — Abba doesn't want robotic believers."

Alejandro sighed and stared out the contrans window. "It would be easier though," he whispered.

Chapter 3

THE NEXT FEW STOPS were much the same. Alejandro was getting more and more dejected and Allie didn't know what to do about it. Nothing she said was helping boost his morale.

They finally got a break at a tiny village, where nearly everyone accepted the Lord's invitation of salvation. Allie and Alejandro were ecstatic and then helped the residents pack their belongings so they could move to the Paradise Gardens, where they'd be safer.

Until Lucifer's war anyway.

Allie didn't admit it, but she was dreading the time they reached the army camp. Abba's words of warning kept haunting her. She didn't have too great a track record when it came to *not* getting captured, and she definitely didn't want to get caught in the midst of the camp while Alejandro was with her.

Lucifer might want her for whatever reason, but she doubted he would play nice when it came to the Chief Witness who was basically telling humanity that Lucifer was a liar.

The devil wasn't known for his kindnesses.

They had similar successes in the next town, a few more failures and disappointments. And then they reached the outskirts of the sprawling city of Mandeville.

Sitting on top of a hill overlooking the city, Allie immediately had a bad feeling about the place, but it was on Abba's map He'd given them of stops, so they had no choice but to go in.

It occurred to her then that this was Abba's plan, to have them start at the smaller villages, et cetera, and get a plan of action in place, to know when things were getting bad enough that they needed to leave, before they ended up surrounded by millions of Lucifer's soldiers.

After moving the contrans behind a hill, they walked in silence down the hill. Even though the vehicle was programmed to her and Alejandro's DNA and no one could steal it, Allie wanted to make sure it was hidden from sight.

It could still be vandalized.

"Hold up," she told Alejandro as he practically ran down the hill. "We need to be smart," she reminded him.

Allie could see him sigh as he turned toward her. The frustration was evident on his face, but their safety came before Alejandro's comfort. Or happiness.

"Let's check the place out first," she suggested. After what had just happened in the village, she assumed that Alejandro would be on board with her decisions.

She was wrong.

"Seriously?" Alejandro huffed as he spun around

from his position down the hill from her. "Do you really think Abba wants us to be fearful?"

Allie shook her head as she moved to stand beside Alejandro. "No. But He does want us to be careful. He told me that."

Alejandro turned back to look down on the town below them. His shoulders heaved as he sighed.

"Yeah, I guess," he murmured. "I suppose we should be careful."

Allie had to fight not to roll her eyes and say, "Ya think? If Abba Himself says 'be careful', then you darned well had better listen." But she managed to make her mouth and eyeballs behave.

"So that means that you need to stay *near me* at all times," Allie told him again. He reluctantly nodded.

She patted her friend on the back, and they continued down the hill. They could see the residents bustling to and fro, going about their daily activities. Allie thought it was so strange how life could just continue to go on status quo, even though the end of the age as they knew it was right over the horizon.

They headed toward the city's gates. That was another thing Allie thought was weird in the New Age — people had built walls and fences around their cities and towns, just like they had many thousands of years before. It was kind of like humanity sort of just started over again. Other than things like the contrans that Abba had created, there was no real technology. No advancements had been made for making life easier and more comfortable.

It was like people had gotten stuck in the Renaissance Period.

Once they were inside the gates, it seemed like someone had called a halt to all movement. The people they'd seen scurrying around stopped in their tracks and stared at the pair as they walked toward the town center. Allie knew a lot of the staring was due to her uniform and the giant shield she was carrying, but probably much of the looks could have been due to the fact that they were just strangers to Mandeville.

"Mistress, Chief Witness," a man greeted them as he stepped forward hesitantly. Allie and Alejandro both nodded in return.

"How may I help you?" He seemed pleasant enough, certainly much nicer than the people at the village had been.

"We are here to speak to your residents," Alejandro told the man, who cocked his head as if waiting for more information.

"Do you have a town square, or a center well?" Allie asked before he started questioning them. He nodded and turned, walking in a westerly direction. The pair followed.

"We don't want any trouble," the man said over his shoulder. Allie knew he was probably afraid she was there to mete out punishment.

"I'm not here in a Remnant capacity," she told him. "Alejandro is here to witness to your population and I'm here for his protection."

The man nodded again, looking relieved. Allie wondered if he had some sin he was hiding. It didn't matter; like she'd told him, she wasn't there in for Remnant duty. The punishment of sins had stopped with Lucifer's releasing. This time was his.

They walked down several streets, their presence stopping the citizens in their tracks as they moved along. Allie noticed that the citizens were more balanced in Mandeville than they were in the village, with a more even distribution of women to men. She then opened her senses, ready to feel the usual malcontent and animosity that she usually sensed in the Inner Circle population, but she was surprised at the lack of both. Most people were just feeling understandably curious. Some were worried.

But most were... hopeful.

That surprised her, but it in turn made her hopeful that they'd have a better time of it there in the larger town.

The man leading them, who had finally introduced himself as Edwan, led them to what was obviously a common area situated in a large courtyard in the midst of tall buildings. There were dozens of people in the area and they all stopped whatever they were doing and turned to follow them toward a platform structure.

Edwan moved to a set of stairs and motioned for

Allie and Alejandro to follow. Once they were on the platform, the man stepped to one side. Alejandro glanced out over the crowd that was growing steadily and quickly.

"I wish to speak to all the townspeople," he told Edwan. "Is it possible to call them together?"

Edwan nodded. "Yes, I will ring the town bell. We rarely use it, only in emergencies, really." A haunted look crossed his face then.

"The last time it was rung was when Lucifer came here, recruiting for his army."

Allie made a *hmm* sound. "Was he able to get a lot of men to join him?" It still galled her that Lucifer only chose men for his army. She knew it was really dumb to feel that way, because less people for the enemy was less people, regardless of their sex. But as a warrior, it didn't sit well with her that women were discriminated against regardless.

She knew that a ticked off woman with a weapon was a very formidable foe.

A ghost of a smile crossed Edwan's face. "Not really. Mandeville has always been... rather neutral."

Alejandro smiled then. Allie knew what he was thinking; neutral wasn't great, but it was better than opposed to Abba at least.

Edwan turned then and walked down the stairs. Allie and Alejandro watched as he made his way across the courtyard to the biggest building, which Allie assumed was some sort of government building.

Most of the towns had some form of government, a mayor, at least, to keep the peace.

Except for the Outer Circle — the communities there were more a free-for-all.

She felt eyes on her and fought the urge to squirm. Allie always hated being the center of attention, despite the show she sometimes put on, that of being the "class clown." She forced herself to stand still and act like a warrior.

It wasn't easy.

Her eyes involuntarily flickered toward the crowd. There wasn't any hostility that she could tell, which was a good thing. After the village, she'd been worried they were going to be met with resistance and anger everywhere they went.

Allie's lips twitched at the corners when she saw a large group of kids standing at the base of the platform, staring up at her in awe. Ever since the Tribulation in the Old Age, when she'd been given the task of watching over the younger children, she'd had a special place in her heart for the little ones.

She dropped her tough chick act and smiled at the kids, then moved to the edge of the platform where they stood. She knelt down on one knee, propping her shield up so that it was easily visible. She loved the shield; not only did it match her sword and uniform, it had a large cross on it, a reminder of what Abba had gone through for humanity in the Old Age.

One little boy was staring at her with a frightened look. Allie figured her was probably four or five years old. She reached down and offered her gloved hand to him, but he just frowned at it. Allie realized he might not think she was really human, what with all the metal on her body.

She pulled her glove off and reached out to him again. When he saw her fingers wiggling at him, he smiled slightly and tentatively reached up to touch her hand. Allie grinned at him and the other kids decided she wasn't so scary after all and they pushed forward to touch her too.

Allie laughed when one of the larger kids tugged on her hand, pulling her slightly off balance. She had to slap her hand down on the platform to keep from toppling off. The kid was surprisingly strong.

"Step back!" a harsh voice barked. The children jumped and stepped back quickly. Allie looked at the crowd and saw a woman pushing her way through, toward the platform. She was scowling, but when she saw Allie's eyes narrowed on her, she smiled.

"I'm so sorry, Mistress," the woman said as she roughly yanked some of the children back from the platform.

"They know better than to bother any of The City's officials."

Allie shook her head. "They weren't bothering me; I came to them. I wanted to say 'hi'."

It took every drop of control Allie had not to leap

off the stage onto the woman when she shoved a little girl behind her, making her fall to the ground with a cry. Allie noticed several people in the crowd scowling at her actions too.

Allie stood then, laying her shield on the floor of the platform. She crossed her arms over her chest and scowled at the woman.

"They're just children. There is no need to be so rough with them." Allie knew her words were biting, just as she meant them to be. The woman flinched slightly, hearing the warning.

But her mean eyes narrowed. "They're my concern, Mistress," she argued. "I am in charge of their well-being and their behavior."

Allie leaned forward slightly and made sure she had the woman's attention… and everyone else within hearing distance, which had grown to quite a few after the confrontation started. People were inherently nosy.

"I believe you need another occupation," Allie said. "Perhaps we should take it up with your superiors."

The woman's eyes widened at the threat, but she didn't look worried. Instead, she seemed to be offering a challenge. She then huffed and turned to herd the children away. Allie watched her, waiting for her to give her a reason to jump off the platform and go after her. If she even looked at one of those children in the wrong way, it was on.

"Not sure threatening the people was on the agenda," Alejandro said dryly from behind her. Allie turned and smirked at him.

"Maybe not, but it was necessary." He nodded in agreement, then laughed and clapped her on the shoulder.

"Nothing has changed in a thousand years," he laughed. "You're still a mama bear with the kids. I remember too well how bossy you can be. You ruined a lot of my fun."

Allie laughed too and punched him lightly in the arm. Alejandro grinned at her and then they both turned when they heard a loud bell coming from the building Edwan had disappeared into. In just a few minutes, the courtyard filled with people.

Which meant even more eyeballs staring her way. Allie was starting to sweat under her uniform.

She wanted to prod Alejandro to hurry up and do his thing so they could get out of there, but she forced herself to be patient, which was never her strongpoint.

Hey Abba... need Your help here. Feeling pretty antsy and ready to grab Andro and bolt.

Immediately, a peaceful feeling came over her. Allie grinned and gave a thumbs up, ignoring the people watching her, trying to figure out what she was doing.

"Thanks, Dad!" she called and almost laughed when she saw people looking around, trying to figure out who she was talking to.

After many more long moments, Alejandro finally started to speak. He basically said the same thing that he had in the village, but this time he kept the emphasis on Abba's goodness and salvation, rather than on the deception of Lucifer, like they'd talked about.

And people listened. Really listened.

When he was done with what turned out to be a fairly simple speech, Alejandro offered to say a prayer for any of those who wanted to accept Abba's salvation offer. Countless hands rose wanting the prayer that Allie nearly fell to her knees in shock. She never would have believed so many people would accept.

Abba triumphed yet again.

Chapter 4

THE PAIR WAS fueled by the success they'd experienced in Mandeville. By the time they'd left the town, hundreds of families were already packed and leaving, heading toward The City. Those who hadn't accepted salvation were being witnessed to by their friends and neighbors, which was both funny and promising.

According to the map, the next stop was another village. After being so warmly welcomed in Mandeville, Allie didn't bother hiding the contrans outside of the village and instead parked right outside the gate.

Unfortunately, their reception wasn't nearly as warm as it had been in the town.

After being practically run out of village, Allie and Alejandro had sped off in the contrans, then stopped among some sand dunes.

"What is it about the villages?" Alejandro griped. "It's like they think they're invincible or something. Makes no sense."

"Yeah," Allie agreed. "Maybe it's because they're so close-knit in the small communities that they all get the same mind set. One decides to side with the enemy, so they all jump in."

Alejandro nodded. "Or maybe they think that

Lucifer won't bother them since they're such a small place." He shook his head sadly.

"I don't want to be there when they find out they're wrong."

The next stop was a slightly larger village, but they didn't have any better luck there. Afterwards, they again stopped somewhere where they could talk and regroup. But mostly they knew they needed to pray.

"Abba, we need Your help here. Running out of ideas for how to reach these stupid people," Allie said. Alejandro snorted.

"While I wouldn't call them 'stupid people'," he added with a smile and a side glance at Allie, "they do need some pushing. More than what I'm capable of, apparently."

They didn't get an answer, but they knew He'd heard. He always heard.

Allie sighed. "Next is Maripa," she said. "Another small village." It was hard not to be despondent, but they were getting very discouraged by the lack of response.

Thankfully, the people of Maripa were receptive to what Alejandro had to say. Without exception, every single person accepted the offer of salvation. With great joy, Allie directed the grateful residents to The City. They immediately started packing their possessions.

It was just the boost she and Alejandro needed.

When they left that village, Allie had laughed and patted Alejandro on the back. "Apparently, we're morons. Seems we were missing the prayer factor before each stop. Duh."

He chuckled. "Yeah, can't argue, especially since I had prayed for help before we stopped in Mandeville, and look what happened there. Go figure. You would think that we, of all people, would know that we need to ask Abba for help whenever we're working for Him."

"Yep," Allie agreed. "Feeling pretty stupid right now." She scrunched up her face and crossed her eyes, making Alejandro laugh.

Before the next stop, they prayed for a long time and had the same results as in Maripa. But then the next two towns they came to ran them off.

"Win some, lose some," Allie sighed after the second town literally chased them out. Alejandro nodded dejectedly. The poor guy took every rejection of Abba's salvation personally, like he hadn't done his job properly. Allie had no idea how to help him, to get him to focus on the next task.

They'd been staying in the contrans most nights since "hospitality" was found too often, but as they moved closer to the Outer Circle, where the army was supposedly making its move, the weather got worse. They knew they'd need to start finding shelter.

One little village of only about a hundred citizens was very welcoming. It was filled with lovely people who had already been saved but had chosen to stay in their small village because they'd considered it "home." They welcomed Allie and Alejandro and begged them to stay.

Allie and Alejandro happily agreed, since the little village was in a fairly central location to the next dozen or so places that they needed to visit. It was a welcome relief — and an answer to prayer — to have somewhere to lay their heads.

The third week after they'd started their journey, they came to the city of Kidal. It was large, with a huge fortified wall built around it.

"Wonder if they're trying to keep people in, or others out," Alejandro muttered as they stared up at the high wall. It reminded Allie of pictures she'd seen in the Old Age, of the walls people of long ago had built around castles.

And just like those pictures, there were even people patrolling along the top, who were staring down at them. It was unnerving, even though Allie knew they wouldn't have weapons, since they were outlawed in the New Age. Of course, rocks were still readily available.

She kept an eye on the guards to make sure they didn't try lobbing a boulder down on their heads.

The gate was closed, so they rang a bell that was attached to the wall. They waited a long time and Alejandro rang it twice more before a little window opened in the wall next to the gate. An angry woman's face appeared in the opening.

"What do you want?" she growled. Allie and Alejandro glanced at each other.

"We wish to speak to your people," Allie told her. "We have an important message."

The woman's eyes traveled up and down her body, obviously taking in the shiny uniform, sword and shield. Allie knew she had to know that she was the Mistress and should be obeyed, but the woman just sneered.

"I don't think so," she huffed and started to close the window, but Allie shoved her gloved hand into the open space.

"You don't have the authority to make that decision," she said with false cheerfulness. "Our orders come from Abba Himself, so I suggest that you open the gate and let us in so that we can complete our mission and that way no one has to suffer any... consequences." She grinned widely at the woman.

While Allie knew it was sort of an empty threat, the woman didn't know that. She made a face that said she didn't like being argued with, but she finally nodded once and then yelled at someone, ordering them to open the gate.

Once they were inside, Allie and Alejandro glanced at each other again as the gate closed behind them. Uneasiness filled her at the thought of being locked inside the unknown city. If they weren't going to be welcomed, she just hoped that they were run off, rather than finding themselves taken captive.

She really hated being a prisoner.

"Stay here," the woman who'd "greeted" them ordered. Allie fought not to smirk at her. She wasn't good at being told what to do. Abba was the only one who got away with ordering her around.

The woman turned and casually strolled off, obviously intent on taking her time. Allie sighed and Alejandro barked out an uneasy laugh. Allie glanced at her friend in question.

"Don't have a good feeling about this one," he muttered. Allie nodded.

"Yeah, no kidding."

After a long while, the woman came back with two men. They were all wore matching scowls; it was obvious playing escort was the last thing they wanted to be doing. Allie didn't care what they thought; she just wanted to get Alejandro to do his thing and get the heck out of the place.

"Follow us," one of the men barked, like they were going to jump to do as he ordered.

Allie's sword hand twitched, wanting to draw her weapon. She managed to keep it in the scabbard. Barely.

The trio led them down one street and up another, making so many turns that Allie was sure they were backtracking. She started to get suspicious that they were purposely being confused so that they wouldn't be able to find the gate again.

Like they planned on keeping them.

Of course, that was a stupid thought, since it was all too obvious that the townspeople wanted nothing to do with them, judging by the glares they were getting as they moved through a particularly populated area. There were hundreds of people in what must have been the city's marketplace.

She realized then that it wasn't just their reluctant guides who were shooting hateful looks their way; men, women and even children were all frowning and sneering as they passed. One older man with what looked like a bad comb-over in particular was looking at them with sheer hatred.

It was unnerving.

Allie was becoming more agitated with each block they crossed, and Alejandro was so stiff from the tension in the air that Allie could swear she would be able to snap him in half. When she laid her hand gently on his shoulder for reassurance, he nearly jumped a foot.

"Easy there, Kemosabe," she joked. Of course, the reference went right over his head. She was usually the only one who ever got her jokes from Old Age television.

"It'll be okay," she told him instead. "Remember, Abba Himself gave us the map of places we're supposed to visit. He decided where we need to go, and if that means we have to be in a huge town surrounded by people who hate our guts and probably want us dead, so be it!" she said with way more enthusiasm than was necessary.

It worked, because Alejandro barked out a laugh and grinned at her. "You're a nut," he muttered as he shook his head.

The group walked for about fifteen minutes until they came to a sprawling building. Like all the other buildings in Kidal, it was only one story. But it was huge, taking up several of the city blocks.

"Wait here," the woman ordered, leaving Allie and Alejandro with the two grumpy men acting as guards. Allie stared at the pair, who just returned her look with a frown.

"Gotta problem with us?" she asked as she crossed her sword arm over her chest and tapped the scabbard where it jutted up over her shoulder. It was a slight threat, and one that the men actually took to heart, when they looked away, unease in their expressions.

That's right, jerks. I'm the only one in the city with a weapon and I ain't afraid to use it.

After another five minutes, the woman returned with a larger group of people. They all looked like self-important officials, the type that Allie couldn't stand. She never could understand why the officials in the Inner Circle and Outer Zone always had to puff themselves up. In Abba's City, none of the officials acted like they were special. In fact, they were much more humble than even the lowest servant.

"What is your business in Kidal?" one of the women in the group asked without even bothering to introduce herself.

Allie grinned at her, showing all her teeth. A totally fake smile.

"Hello," she said pleasantly, like they'd just showed up for tea. "I'm Alessandra, Mistress of the Remnant Warriors, and this is Alejandro, Chief Witness to Those Born During the New Age."

The group's mutual frowns turned to scowls. "We know who you are," the woman snapped. She was apparently the spokesperson for the grouchy group.

"I asked, what is your business here?"

Allie sighed and rolled her eyes. She was tired of being treated with such hatred and disrespect, but she was somewhat used to it. Alejandro, however, was not, and that they would treat him like that angered her more than anything else.

"We have a message for your city," she barked at them. "A message from Abba. It's *His* mission we're on," she stressed, hoping that knowing the Creator Himself had sent them would hold some merit.

"What is this message?" the woman snapped again. Allie glanced at Alejandro, whose face mirrored the concern she felt. Apparently, even knowing that it was Abba's mission they were on meant nothing.

Not a good sign.

"Look, can you just direct us to the center of your city, or wherever people gather when you have something important to impart to them? We just want to get this over with and get out of your hair."

The woman's frown deepened again. Allie didn't know if it was because she was being pushier than the woman would have liked, or if it was due to Allie's terminology. Probably the latter.

Without another word, she turned her back on them and the rest of the group gathered around her. They started conferring with one another, murmuring so low that most wouldn't be able to hear them. But not Allie; thanks to her status, she had enhanced senses and she heard every word they spoke.

And as soon as she'd heard enough, she grabbed Alejandro by the shoulder and transferred them back to the marketplace they'd passed. It seemed to be where the most people had been gathered.

Alejandro's head wobbled a little and he looked shocked by the sudden transfer, but Allie couldn't waste any time consoling him.

"Hurry up and say what you need to. Make it real quick, too, cuz these bozos are planning on capturing us and holding us for ransom."

His eyes bugged, but he nodded and jumped up on a low wall and started his shouting testimony.

"Friends, we have a message for you from The Creator Himself. I must make this quick, because your officials do not want you to hear this message, but it concerns your eternity. Where you will spend it..."

He then gave them the truth, but it was obvious it was falling on deaf ears. And the message was making them angry, judging by the snarls and head shaking going on.

Allie kept her eyes on the huge crowd that had gathered, waiting for someone, anyone, to make any sort of movement that could be construed as an attack. She reached back to grab her sword and put her other hand out to grab Alejandro to get them out of there.

Unfortunately, she didn't notice who was behind her.

Chapter 5

ALLIE JERKED AT the familiar feeling of a shackle snapping on her wrist. She spun around to see the man with the bad comb-over grinning at her. Allie snarled in response, then grabbed Alejandro by the shoulder to transfer them to safety again.

Only... nothing happened.

The man laughed at her and Allie glanced down at her wrist. A long chain hung from the shackle, to where another open shackle lay in the dirt. She frowned at her wrist as she tried to open the latch. It didn't budge.

Great. Just great. There was only one thing that could keep her from transferring, and that was a shackle from The Pit. But that made no sense; the shackles could only be attached, or removed, by an angel and the man laughing at her at the moment was no angel. *In fact...*

"Demon," she breathed.

The man laughed. "Very good, Mistress."

Allie took a stumbling step backward and almost fell, but Alejandro grabbed her arm to steady her. The demon laughed even harder.

"How... what..." she shook her head to clear it. She couldn't get the words she needed to say out.

"How is this possible?" she demanded to know, reclaiming her authority. Allie knew in the situation, she'd better act like the tough chick she was supposed to be, even if she wasn't feeling it at the moment. She held her wrist up and shook the chain for emphasis, wincing at the realization that it was attached to her sword arm.

The demon shrugged, crossing his arms over his chest as he released the disguise he'd been holding over himself, revealing a large, muscular — and unfortunately, handsome — man.

"The shackles are made from metal that comes from The Pit, but they were not forged by The Creator."

"Great, just freaking great," Allie mumbled. That meant that Lucifer had once again tried to copy Abba, this time by creating his own shackles, which apparently could only be attached by demons.

Eyes on the demon, she reached out and grabbed Alejandro by the back of his tunic and started pulling him away. The chain dragged along the ground behind him, tripping him every few steps, but Allie kept tugging her friend. With her free hand, she pulled her sword from its scabbard.

That action made the demon stop smiling and start snarling.

Alejandro finally seemed to recover from his shock when he turned and grabbed the chain hanging from Allie's wrist and started running. Of course, she had no choice but to follow.

Allie hated to run from a fight, but she knew that she wouldn't be very effective protecting Alejandro by trying to fight off the huge crowd with the stupid heavy and long chain hanging from her sword arm.

They didn't get very far before the crowd surged around them. Allie awkwardly swung her sword and chain, warning the others off, before she switched hands. She wasn't as effective with her other hand, but she was still deadly regardless.

The crowd didn't seem to care though. They kept closing in, closer and closer. Allie wondered then if the demon had some sort of an influential power.

She'd always thought that it sucked that Abba allowed demons to have some powers. It certainly leveled the playing field with the Remnants and angels and, while she didn't like it, she knew that Abba was always about being fair and balanced.

A man approached, a menacing look on his face. Allie swung her sword in an effort to keep him away, but the chain tangled around her legs and knocked her off balance. She fell back into Alejandro, knocking them back against the low wall. They tumbled over it and Allie landed on top of Alejandro, probably knocking the wind out of the poor guy.

Allie cursed her clumsiness, even though she knew it was due to the stupid chain. She had to figure out how to fight without tripping over it. Before she could crawl off Alejandro, she was hit in the head from behind.

Stars exploded in her vision and she gritted her

teeth, willing herself to stay conscious. Before she could get a grip on the pain and turn around to fight off her attacker, another blow came from the side, right to her ribs that had just healed not too long before.

She felt them crack again.

Alejandro yelled a warning right in her ear, but Allie couldn't do much to fight off any more attacks. She gave up trying to get off of her friend, and instead used her body to protect him.

At least one of them might make it out alive.

But then someone yanked Alejandro out from under her. Allie cried out and grabbed for her friend, but she missed. She watched helplessly as he was hauled away, yelling her name and struggling against his attackers.

The attack on her seemed to increase in intensity then. Allie clenched her jaw to keep from crying out as she felt the blows and kicks connecting. Thanks to training with the Remnants she was used to pain, but not that much at one time.

And at that moment, her entire body felt like it was broken.

Just before she passed out from the agony racing through her body and gave in to the dark oblivion of unconsciousness, Allie could have sworn she heard a lion roaring.

Chapter 6

ALLIE MOANED AS consciousness returned. Every bone, muscle, and stinking blood vessel in her body ached and she wondered what ox cart had run her over. Her memory was fuzzy, and her head was pounding like her skull had been split open.

She was lying on her side on some sort of mat, her back to a wall. Struggled to push herself to a sitting position, groaning at the agony that slammed into her at the movement. Once she was finally upright, she slumped back against the wall and cried out at the contact. Her back felt like she'd been whipped, plus she was pretty sure her ribs were broken, along with one of her legs.

It was like a repeat of the time she'd been thrown in The Pit, but at least then she'd been under a paralysis power and hadn't felt her injuries.

Dang it. Captured again. It was becoming an ongoing theme with her.

But how had she been captured? And when? She couldn't even remember what she'd been doing... before. Before whatever it was that had happened to put her in the situation she now found herself in. It was strange, not being able to remember.

Trying to shake the confusion from her mind, she glanced around. She was in some sort of cell.

Underground, judging by the musty smell. It might have even been a cave.

It was dark, but not completely black. There was some light source somewhere, off in the distance from what she could tell. At least it wasn't totally dark.

Allie remembered something then... scripture said something about spending eternity in utter darkness if you chose not to follow Abba. A painful shudder racked her damaged body.

She hated the dark.

A need for comfort had her reaching out with her mind. *Abba, help me. What happened? Where am I? Kinda freaking out here...*

With sudden clarity, Allie remembered that she and Alejandro had been in Kidal, that the people were hateful, filled with animosity. She'd heard them conspiring to capture her and Alejandro...

But she'd transferred them, hadn't she? She tried to concentrate on bringing her memories together, ignoring the pain in her brain at the effort. She remembered knowing that the city elders had wanted to capture them, and she'd wanted to get Alejandro away, but she knew they still had a mission to complete.

The Chief Witness still had to do his witnessing.

She remembered taking him back to the marketplace where it seemed most of the city had gathered. Alejandro had started doing his thing and then... they'd been attacked.

No, that wasn't right. She shook her head slightly, trying to remember. The crowd had been hostile, she remembered. She knew they didn't want to hear any convicting words. She'd reached for her sword just as a defense, just in case...

And a demon had put a shackle on her.

Allie looked down at her wrist. The shackle was still attached, the long chain length still hanging from it. She was a bit surprised that she wasn't chained to the wall, but then with her injuries, she definitely wasn't going to get far in any escape attempt. Allie snorted to herself; she wouldn't even make it to the cell door in her condition.

She carefully lifted the arm with the shackle and stared at the chain. She suddenly remembered getting tangled in the chain and knocking Alejandro down. Before she could get back up, though, the crowd had attacked. They'd beaten her senseless, apparently literally.

Alejandro had been dragged off, screaming. Her heart clenched at the thought of her friend being captured. Allie knew she might be getting used to being held captive, but he definitely wasn't.

Other than the brief time he'd been captured in Kingston after The Releasing, the Chief Witness had never been subjected to anything like the stuff Allie had been through. Besides the time she'd spent in captivity, she'd trained, fought and been injured countless times with the Remnants.

But Alejandro had lived out the entire Millennium in the comforts of The City and had only traveled out of The City's protection to witness to the lost back before The Releasing, when the Remnants were still meting out punishment.

When the world had still been fairly safe.

"Alejandro?" she croaked out, surprised at how scratchy her throat was. *How long have I been here?* she wondered when she realized she was seriously thirsty. It must have been quite a while.

Her heart pounded to match her head when she got no answer from her friend. Despair crept its way into her mind when she started fearing for her friend's welfare. It had been up to her to protect him, but she'd failed. Allie wanted to scream in frustration.

Allie really, *really* hated to fail. Especially when it meant others got hurt.

She tried to transfer but remembered the chain on her wrist was made of the same metal that Lucifer had used to keep her bound. Which meant Lucifer was probably behind her capture.

Again.

"Hello?" she called out. "Really thirsty here. Can I get some water?" Her voice was barely more than a croak.

There was no answer. No sound at all.

"Abba, I could use your help!" she shouted,

ignoring the pain that racked her brain as she did so. She was desperate for help.

"These idiots you sent us to witness to have captured us!" Silence greeted her.

She knew that He was well aware of what was going on, but just like the other times she'd been captured, she had no idea why He'd allowed it.

Allie sighed and tried to calm herself. Panicking wouldn't solve anything, she knew. Of course, that didn't stop her heart from racing and her breaths from coming in short bursts. She huffed out a harsh breath and tried to calm herself.

It didn't work.

Just when she thought her brains were going to squeeze out of her ears thanks to the pounding in her head, she heard a slight shuffling sound and she froze when the cell door creaked opened and a pair of massive shoulders pushed through the opening

In the New Age everyone was pretty much the same size. But for some reason, the guy now standing in her tiny cell hadn't gotten that memo. The dude was freaking huge.

And since she was so helpless, that scared the heck out of her.

Chapter 7

L ET ME GUESS," Allie rasped, "Goon Squad?"

The man cocked his head to the side and grinned slightly. "No, I'm Duward. I have food for you."

Allie's eyes traveled over his massive frame. In addition to the cell being dimly lit, Duward was so dark that she couldn't make out his features, only the whites of his eyes and the flash of white teeth when he spoke.

She tried opening her senses to see if he meant her any harm, but she felt nothing. If the chain on her wrist had truly come from The Pit, then she wouldn't be able to use any of her powers.

"Oh. Sorry Duward," she croaked. "I just figured you were here to beat me until I talked."

Even in the darkness, Allie could tell she'd shocked the guy. "I would never hurt you," he grumbled, like she'd just insulted him.

"Okay. Sorry again, but you gotta know that I had no way of knowing that." Her voice was getting even scratchier and Duward turned and bent to pick something up off the floor by the metal door.

Which he'd left open.

Allie contemplated if she could escape then, if she could somehow get her injured arms to work so that she could wrap a chain around Duward's neck and choke him out. She didn't want to kill the guy, but just knock him out so she could escape. But then she remembered that she was too injured to do much more than moan.

Duward stood then and retrieved what looked like a wineskin. He held it while she took a hesitant sip. She almost groaned when she realized it was just cool water. Allie was so thirsty that she drank half of it before getting her fill.

The giant man ran a gentle thumb over her chin, wiping away the water she'd dribbled. It was such a sweet gesture. He then turned and picked up a plate and she watched as he tore off some bread, feeding it to her like she was an infant.

Up close, Allie could see the man had kind eyes, despite his size. He was the kind of man she would have crossed the street, ran down an alley and climbed a fence to avoid in the Old Age. Just huge and scary looking.

Of course, that was back when she judged people by their looks without knowing them and she knew better now.

It also made her realize how much she relied on her special ability to sense the intention of sin in others. The ability had come in handy over the Millennium, knowing what others were planning on doing, what evil they held in their hearts. Wrapped in Lucifer's chain, though, she was left to figure it out on her own.

And she was pretty sure Duward was a good guy.

"How long have I been here?" she asked between bites of bread and some sort of roasted vegetable. Even sitting on the floor in front of her, he towered over her and she had to crane her stiff, sore neck to see his face.

"It has been three days since I brought you here. This is the first time you have awakened."

Allie's mouth opened in shock and Duward used the opportunity to feed her more bread.

After swallowing, she asked, "Have you seen my companion... Alejandro?"

Duward nodded, then glanced toward the door. He leaned a little closer. "Your friend is fine. I helped him escape this morning. The others are out searching for him now, so I was able to bring you food."

Allie smiled at that; knowing that Alejandro had escaped was a huge relief. "Thank you," she told her new friend.

He shook his head, a sad look on his face. "Don't thank me. I should have done something sooner, to prevent this," he muttered as he waved at her body. Allie assumed he meant her injuries.

Allie's eyes roamed over the big guy. His muscles had muscles. He looked as strong as a grizzly. A memory of a lion roaring flitted through her mind and she knew with sudden clarity that Duward had come to her rescue.

"You saved me," she murmured.

Duward glanced up at her from where he was tearing off another piece of bread. His eyes again moved to her body and he winced, then nodded reluctantly.

"Not soon enough," he growled, "and for that I am truly sorry."

Allie shook her head in denial but moaned at the sharp pain that motion caused. She wondered if she had some broken vertebrae and tried to reach up to her neck, but her arms were pretty useless.

Duward leaned forward then, so close his chest brushed her face. His big hands moved gently around her neck as he felt for injuries. He grunted at whatever he found.

He smelled like the outdoors, which in Allie's mind was the smell of heaven at the moment. She hated the muskiness of the cell. It reminded her too much of her time in The Pit.

"Are we underground? Like in a cave or something?"

Duward leaned back and nodded. "Yes, this is the prison and it's under the Kidal Council Building, which was built on top of a mountain. I brought you here because I knew they would never think to look for you in this place."

Allie frowned at that. Almost every building in the Inner Circle and Outer Zone had been built after the events of the Tribulation had destroyed just about everything. So that meant that the people in Kidal had built a prison, which made no sense, because the people weren't supposed to punish their own; that was the Remnants' job.

She looked back at her new friend. He had a smirk on his face, like he knew she'd just figured it out. "That's right, Mistress, the people of this city have gone against Abba from the beginning."

"But why didn't Abba stop them?" Allie asked. She knew it was a question that neither she nor Duward would be able to answer.

He was smart enough to not bother trying to answer. Instead, he set the plate of food on her lap and then reached for her shackled wrist. The massive muscles in his arms bulged as he pulled at the metal and Allie knew if it had been made of a "normal" material, the shackle wouldn't have stood a chance.

"Don't bother," she told him. "It was apparently made by Lucifer, and only a demon can open it." She wondered if her angel friends would be able to remove it though.

Duward scowled at the shackle as if it offended him that it wouldn't bow to his wishes. He sighed then and gently put her wrist back into her lap.

"Well, you will still be able to escape the city, but you'll be dragging the chain with you."

Allie laughed softly, wincing at the pain in her ribs. "I'm just glad to know that I'm not a captive. As long as I can get out of here, I don't care. I can use the chain as a weapon."

She frowned then. "Speaking of, do you know where my sword and shield went?" She was thankful she at least still had her armor on, especially since she wasn't wearing much underneath. Being a captive was bad enough but being a naked captive would have really sucked.

Duward nodded. "I put them in the armory," he murmured. "For safekeeping."

Armory? Other than the Remnants, no one was allowed to have weapons in the New Age.

"Why in the world would there be an armory?" she practically yelled.

He gave her a look. "Like we've already discussed, the people of Kidal are not exactly obedient."

Allie huffed. "True, but knowing they're keeping weapons makes me wonder even more why Abba allowed it."

Duward shrugged his massive shoulders, apparently done with the conversation. He stepped over her then, so that he was straddling her body. Allie leaned as far back as she could, because it was a very... intimate position. Not to mention super awkward.

He leaned down to scoop her up, but like hers had before, his feet tangled in her chain and he fell back, hitting the stone floor with a thud.

"Are you okay?" Allie asked.

Duward winced but laughed. "My tailbone may have a bruise, but it's nothing compared to your injuries, little warrior."

The nickname made her smile. It was what Metatron always called her. But Duward's comment made her frown. She looked down at her leg that was most likely broken, judging by the pain she felt with the slightest movement. Her ribs too. The possible broken vertebrae in her back and neck and the unknown injuries causing the weakness in her arms.

Her eyes met Duward's worried ones. "I'll be all right, big guy. I've had worse," she laughed. It was true. She'd been sliced open, broken and beaten over the past thousand years. And even before the Millennium.

She just never had so many injuries all at one time.

"If I can find my companion, we have a healing rod in our contrans." It was something Abba had required, and He gave her the healing power needed to use it. At the moment she was thankful He had insisted. Of course, He probably knew she'd be injured.

Of course He knew... duh.

Allie started to push herself up, but Duward put a hand on her shoulder.

"I will carry you," the man announced. Allie laughed.

"Be careful of the chain," she warned, a little too late.

Duward scowled at her, but he reached for the chain and tossed it over his shoulder, then lifted her easily, cradling her like a child. At first, the pressure on her ribs was unbearable, but he carefully adjusted her and the pain lessened to a point she could breathe again.

He turned then and carried her out the door and into the hallway that looked more like something you'd see in a mine than a basement. He started jogging down the long hall, so smoothly that Allie was barely jostled.

"Can we get my sword and shield?" Allie asked as they approached a set of stairs.

Duward glanced down at her and then nodded. "The armory isn't guarded, and since most of the officials are looking for your companion, it should be safe."

At that reminder, Allie grimaced, feeling guilty for being self-absorbed. *Abba, please keep Alejandro safe and out of enemy hands.*

As if it took no effort at all, Duward took the stairs two at a time. Allie was amazed; the guy was as strong as the angels.

"Are you an angel?" she voiced her thoughts.

Duward looked down at her with worry etching his face. "No... are you getting delirious, little warrior?"

Allie grunted. "Nah. Just trying to figure out why you're helping me."

The corner of his mouth lifted. "Because you are the Mistress, because you are on Abba's side and because no one deserves to be beaten by so many like you were."

Those were good enough reasons for her.

They reached the top of the stairs and the big man turned left, jogging down another short hallway to a door, which he kicked open. Allie started to suggest they make sure no one was inside before barging in, but they were in the room before she could get a single word out.

The room was most definitely an armory. Allie's wide eyes took in the huge assortment of weapons — bows and arrows, swords, knives, spears and axes. Shockingly, there were even some firearms from the Old Age.

"What the—" she breathed as she stared at all the rifles lining one wall.

Duward shrugged, the movement jostling her a bit. "They were found in a vault in the mountain."

Allie's wide eyes took in the vast assortment of weaponry. She hadn't seen anything like it since the Old Age when she had stolen from an enemy armory.

Some boxes in the corner caught her attention and Duward followed her eyes. She turned to him with a wide stare.

"Explosive plastics?" she breathed. How in the world explosives had survived a thousand years without blowing the city to bits was beyond her.

Duward shrugged again. "This was a gold mine in the Old Age. My father worked here then. He told me stories of the poor treatment from the mine owners."

Allie's eyes traveled over the weapons again. "I'm thinking the place was used for more than just mining gold."

He nodded. "The mine supported some rebel group. I suppose these weapons were theirs."

Allie stared up at him. "It's amazing that they're still intact," she murmured.

"They were found in a concrete vault," he said by way of explanation. "I guess it was enough to keep the decay at bay."

Allie nodded. "Do you think they still work?"

The big guy shook his head. "I have no idea. I wouldn't even know how to use them."

Allie laughed. "I do. I shot a lot of firearms in the Old Age."

Duward's eyebrows rose and a grin spread across his face, showing stark white teeth against his midnight skin.

"Let's find out if they're good then."

Chapter 8

AFTER GATHERING AS many weapons as they could carry — well, mostly Allie was doing the weapon carrying, since Duward was doing the injured person carrying — they exited the council building through a backdoor and Duward ran for the treeless hills behind the place.

It was nearly the same place where Allie and Alejandro had left the contrans. Allie started to call out for her friend but remembered that Duward had warned her to be quiet before they left the council building, since there were searchers out looking for Alejandro.

"Over there," she whispered as she pointed with her chin since her hands were full. Duward turned in the direction she indicated

When she saw the contrans, Allie didn't know if she should be relieved or worried. She was glad she'd be able to use the healing rod stored in the hidden compartment under the backseat, but she was also worried that Alejandro hadn't taken the vehicle to escape.

Duward ran toward it and Allie asked him to carry her to the back, where she carefully set their stolen weapons, then she reached out and placed her palm on the vehicle, releasing the protective barrier. With the barrier in place, no one else but she or Alejandro would have been able to access it.

Her new friend placed her carefully in the passenger seat, then retrieved the healing rod from its hidden compartment that Allie showed him. Duward then watched as Allie used it on her leg first, since that was causing her the most pain.

But it didn't work.

"Ugh! My powers are blocked by this stupid shackle!" she cried out in frustration, before remembering they were supposed to be quiet. They both quickly scanned the area for approaching enemy, but thankfully all was quiet.

She sighed and ran a hand over her face, cringing when the chain dangling from her wrist slid across her lap. It felt like a heavy snake slithering across her body. She looked at Duward.

"Can you grab the weapons?" He hurried to do as she asked, then placed them in the backseat.

"You're gonna have to drive," she told him and almost laughed when his dark skin paled to a cocoa color.

"I've never—"

Allie waved her hand, interrupting him. "Obviously. Only The City residents have access to the contrans. But it's easy; I'll help you. Get in."

Duward proved to be a natural at driving. He drove them to a hilly area at the outer edge of the Inner Circle, much too far for anyone from Kidal to reach on foot. Allie then relaxed and moved into the spirit.

She sought out her angel friends. Metatron and Zad were training with the Remnants on Shadar, the planet they used for training. She saw her husband and her heart clenched with longing. Nick was in the middle of a fake battle with Evan, and Allie watched for a few moments. She then moved to the edge of the arena, where the angels stood.

Most of the angels didn't seem to be aware of her presence, but as soon as she got close to her best friends, Metatron tensed. It wasn't even a blink of time before he appeared before her in the spiritual realm.

"Little warrior. How are you?" The angel's deep voice filled her mind, even though no actual words were spoken. She'd visited him in the spirit just a few nights before, but the sight of her friend made her want to weep. In fact, she could swear she felt a tear run down her cheek in her physical body.

"Hey guys," she smiled. *"Alejandro and I were attacked by a mob in Kidal but escaped."* She didn't want to go into all the details at the moment; that was a conversation for later.

"Unfortunately, I managed to get another Pit shackle attached to me and now I can't heal myself."

The angels frowned. *"How did you escape a mob if you're injured?"*

Allie shrugged her ghostly shoulders. At least she couldn't feel pain from her injuries while in the spirit.

"Had help from a huge guy. Long story. Anyway, I hate to ask, but could one of you come to me, just long enough to get the shackle off? Abba gave me healing powers, but I obviously can't use them to heal myself with this stupid metal bracelet. Just pop in, release me and pop out."

She wasn't sure, but she thought Zad snorted at that.

"Pop in and out? What are we, ghosts?" he asked. Yep, must have been a snort.

Allie smirked. "Just need your help for a second."

Zad was still snickering and Metatron shot him a look, then turned back to her.

"Yes, little warrior, we will help you. Of course."

She'd barely gotten a "thank you" out when she was aware of Duward sucking in a breath beside her physical body. Allie left the spirit realm to find Duward nearly climbing into her lap as he stared at the massive celestial beings standing next to the contrans. She chuckled; she hadn't expected them to transfer immediately.

Allie patted Duward's arm in an attempt to reassure him. "These are my best friends, Zadkiel and Metatron. Guys, this is Duward. He rescued me," she added, mostly because Metatron was doing his usual scowling and Duward looked like he wanted to crawl under the seat.

The angels nodded to the man in greeting and Duward nodded back, almost automatically, relaxing slightly, though he still seemed to be completely in awe. Allie laughed, even though it made her ribs hurt. She patted him on the shoulder, grimacing when the chain clunked against the seat.

"It's okay, big guy. They're angels."

"Obviously," Duward breathed, then shook his head. "I've never seen angels before."

Huh. It had never occurred to Allie that there might be people who hadn't seen the Heavenly Host. She looked back at her friends with new eyes and realized that, yeah, they were pretty impressive. She thought back to the Tribulation when she'd first seen Zad in his "normal" angelic form and remembered being totally freaked out. So, of course it stood to reason that Duward would be a bit wiggy at seeing them too.

Wait 'til he sees them in their two-story mega angel form, Allie snickered to herself.

She held her hand up. "Can you release me, please?" she wheezed, her ribs screaming from the weight of her arm plus the heavy chain. She wasn't sure if the angels *could* release the shackle, but it was worth a try.

Zad frowned when he realized she was in pain and he reached over Duward to clasp the shackle. Allie waited for the familiar "clink" of it being released. She'd grown to crave that sound when Lucifer had held her captive and would only allow her to be partially unshackled for brief periods of time. He'd always made sure at least one wrist or ankle remained locked down, though, to keep her from using any powers.

A wrinkle marred her angel friend's brow. His startling blue eyes found hers. "It won't release," he said with confusion. Metatron made a huffing sound and pushed his companion to the side.

"Let me," he growled and then gently took Allie's wrist in his huge hands. The same look that Zad just had crossed his face.

He then looked at Duward, who had shrunk back against his seat when the angels had leaned into the contrans.

"What are these are made from?" he snarled at the guy.

Duward's mouth flopped open like a gasping fish and Allie took pity on him. "Be nice," she scolded the angel. "Duward rescued me. Alejandro too, but we don't know where he is." She sighed heavily then.

"They're from The Pit," she explained, rubbing a weary hand over her face with her free hand. Getting confirmation that the angels couldn't release the shackle had been discouraging, to say the least.

"Apparently, Lucifer made them himself, so only demons can operate them. I was afraid of that, but it was worth a try."

Metatron frowned at Allie, obviously not liking the situation any more than she did. He then looked back at Duward, then straightened to his impressive height. Allie almost laughed when Duward released the breath he must have been holding. The angel nodded to the man.

"My apologies for being abrupt," Metatron said, shocking Allie. She didn't think the angel was capable of apologizing to humans.

Duward shook his head a bit dazedly. "It's alright," he mumbled, then glanced back at Allie.

"Supposedly, there were many other shackles created like this one that have been distributed throughout the Circle and Zone."

Both the angels frowned at that.

"What?" Allie asked, starting to worry even more. She was fighting the disappointment from discovering the angels couldn't release her. She'd really hoped they would be able to release her immediately, like Serariel had done for her so many times when she'd been with Lucifer. He had been acting as a "double-agent" angel, pretending to be rebelling against Abba, but had been acting under the Creator's orders to infiltrate the enemy's camp.

Serariel had sacrificed his freedom to save her. As always, whenever she thought of him, Allie's chest hurt at the idea of him hanging in The Pit at that moment.

Metatron closed his eyes and pinched his nose. It was a very human gesture.

"I am sure Lucifer had them created after it was

discovered Serariel was still on Abba's side. He probably fears that more of the angels who claimed to side with him are infiltrators."

Allie cocked her head. "So why would he have a bunch created and sent throughout the badlands? The fallen angels are always with Lucifer." She winced when she realized what she'd said and glanced at Duward. The "badlands" were his home after all.

"Sorry about the 'badlands' comment," she muttered.

He shrugged, his dark eyes twinkling. "No offense was taken. They aren't exactly 'good lands' after all," he smirked.

Zad huffed out a breath then, drawing their attention to him. "Do you really have to ask why Lucifer would have distributed them?" he asked Allie.

He swept his hand toward her. "It was so you could be captured again. No matter where you go, there's a chance that some of those stupid chains will be waiting for you."

Metatron's lips twitched. "Of course, that does not really matter now, since you're already wearing Lucifer's jewelry."

"More like Loserfer," Allie grumbled. "I'm sick of being the deer in his sights. Seriously."

The thought that Lucifer was planning on recapturing her wasn't sitting well, obviously. They hadn't exactly left on the best of terms. For some reason, he hadn't taken kindly to her beating the crap out of him and then before she escaped, she'd witnessed to those Lucifer had planned on talking into following him.

It made her wonder why Abba wanted to send her on the mission to witness to the army. He of course knew everything that was going to happen, and once again, she found herself questioning His motives. But every time anything "bad" had happened to her, it had turned out for the good. Allie wondered what good was going to come out of this situation.

And then her eyes were drawn to Duward. Maybe all of this was just for him, so that he'd be saved. Only one out of the hundreds of thousands in Kidal.

But Abba would do anything to save that one lost sheep.

She smiled to herself. She still didn't know what purpose being shackled would serve, which rendered her basically useless, but she knew it wouldn't do any good to fight against whatever future Abba had in store for her. It didn't stop her from griping though.

"Lovely," she continued to grumble as she leaned back and closed her eyes. "But then, why not? If something can cause me grief or mess me up somehow, then it's going to."

"Murphy's Law," Duward said.

Allie opened her eyes and looked at him. "Right?

Story of my life, all thousand plus years of it." She huffed out a laugh. "I just hope the rest of eternity goes better for me."

Metatron opened his mouth, most likely to give her a lecture on how great eternity would be, but Allie held up a hand. "I know, big guy. I know. I'm just griping." She looked between him and Zad, who was standing with his arms crossed, looking very unhappy about the situation.

Makes two of us buddy.

"So, do either of you two have healing powers?"

The angels shook their heads, both with a look on their face that said they weren't used to being helpless.

"Great. Just great," she muttered. It looked like she was going to be stuck with a broken body and the darned headache.

"Um, I should have said something sooner, but I have healing abilities," Duward murmured, surprising Allie. "My mother was a healer and she taught me too."

She cocked her head at him, then glanced at the angels. "Do you think a mortal human would be able to heal me?"

Zad smirked, finally breaking his silence. "Did you forget the stories of the apostles in the early church? How they healed the lame, the blind, the diseased? Humans with the Holy Spirit have always been able to heal," he shrugged. "It was just something that was forgotten over the ages."

Allie grinned at him, embarrassed. "Oh yeah, duh."

She then looked back at Duward. The Holy Spirit no longer inhabited humans in the New Age, but hopefully he might be able to heal her regardless. It was worth a try.

"Okay big guy," she said as she jerked her thumb toward the healing rod in the backseat. "See what you can do."

He reached back and picked up the rod, handling it like it was an explosive or something. Allie laughed.

"You just tossed firearms around like they were toys and now you're afraid of something that actually heals?" she teased and swore she could almost see the blush that traveled up his neck then.

Duward's lips twitched in a near-smile. "How do I use it?"

"You just hold it over the injury and think about healing it. Concentrate on bones being knit together, flesh mending, that kinda stuff."

Duward turned his big body toward her and then leaned over to hold the wand above her leg. Allie tried to turn to make it easier on him, but the pain at the movement ripped through her and she almost passed out.

"Hold still," Metatron ordered. He sounded like

he was in pain himself and Allie opened her eyes to see that he had moved to her side of the contrans. She reached up and took his hand.

She closed her eyes again and concentrated on healing her leg. Even though the shackle was preventing her powers from working, she figured it wouldn't hurt. She imagined the bones coming together, aligning once again, the vessels and flesh mending, the leg growing stronger than ever.

In just a few moments, she felt warmth spreading through her body and she knew that the healing rod was working in Duward's hands. It was rather amazing that a human could heal like that, could use a celestial creation without any training. Even though the healers were technically human too, they were already immortal, having come through the Tribulation as believers. Duward, and others like him, were born during the Millennium and while they had incredibly long lifespans, they were mortal.

That wouldn't change until Judgment Day.

Allie felt warmth on her side then and knew he was moving the rod over her torso. She wasn't sure if her ribs were broken again, but they were bruised for sure. She probably had an organ or two that needed mending.

He then moved to her head and the headache that had been throbbing behind her eyes disappeared almost immediately. Her body was mended, pain free.

Allie breathed a sigh of relief and opened her

eyes. She smiled at Duward; the look on his face was one of pure concentration. Impulsively, she grabbed him by the cheeks and planted a kiss on him.

"Thanks, sweetie," she told him, laughing at the shocked look on his face. Even though it was common for the residents of The City and the Gardens to give each other a friendly kiss, it wasn't something that was done in the Circle and Zone.

She sighed when the chain banged on her thighs when she released Duward's face. "Now if we could just get my jewelry off..."

The angels matched her sigh with their own. "Other than finding a demon and forcing him to remove them, I'm afraid you're stuck with the chain kiddo," Zad told her. "But the good news is, you won't be alone. Metatron and I are going with you from now on."

"Me too," Duward said enthusiastically, before his ebony eyes darted to Allie. "If that's okay."

Allie smiled fondly at her new friend. "Yes, absolutely," she told him as she squeezed his huge shoulder. She then looked at her angel friends.

"And *heck no* you two aren't coming! I'm not going to let you get in trouble with Abba just so you can babysit me." She shook her head vehemently. "No way."

Metatron rolled his eyes. Allie couldn't help but choke out a laugh. The usually somber angel was becoming more and more human like, which would tick him off if she mentioned it. But he was certainly more personable than he'd ever been before. More like Zad. Metatron was spending too much time with humans, apparently.

And now he was insisting on spending even more.

"We are ready to accept whatever Abba deems as necessary punishment for us," Metatron said in his usual overly formal way, "so do not bothering trying to dissuade us from joining you. You are stuck with us." He crossed his arms while a very stubborn look came over him. Zad nodded enthusiastically in agreement.

Allie rolled her eyes and glanced at Duward. "Let me tell you the first thing about angels. They don't listen to us humans. Like ever. Stubborn jerks. They're gonna get into so much trouble," she moaned.

Zad laughed at her muttered griping as both angels climbed into the back of the contrans. Metatron leaned forward and ruffled her hair, which was so completely unlike him that she turned and stared at him with wide eyes.

"For you, little warrior, we will do anything."

Chapter 9

BY THE FOURTH pass around the area and still no sign of Alejandro, Allie was starting to panic. She was worried that he'd been captured again, but she didn't know what to do about it.

Before they'd started out, she'd asked the angels if they could transfer to Alejandro, but even as the words left her mouth she knew it wasn't possible. In order to transfer to a person, you had to have a connection to them, a sort of intimacy. The angels had little, if anything, to do with Chief Witness. It sure would have made finding him a lot easier than making circles around the same area over and over again.

"Maybe we should circle the mountain one more time," she murmured to Duward. The guy had been enjoying driving the contrans so much that Allie hadn't bothered to take over. Besides, with her improved vision she was able to watch the landscape for signs of her lost friend and not having to watch where she was going was a big help.

Duward turned the contrans back toward the mountain while Zad grumbled. "We should just go back to Kidal and make them tell us where Andro is. And Metatron and I can grab your demon buddy and make him take the shackle off."

Allie turned in her seat to glare at the angel. "If we go back there and you do your Go-Go-Gadget giant thing, Abba is *really* going to be ticked off at you! It's bad enough y'all are insisting on going with us and I'll be darned if I let you stick your necks out any farther for me!"

She huffed as she turned back around. While she appreciated the angels' willingness to help her, she certainly didn't want to be the cause for Abba punishing them. But like she'd told Duward, they were stubborn creatures.

As they passed the same hill for the fifth time, something caught her eye. Darker than the rest of the sandy hill, it looked almost like a shadow.

She tapped Duward's arm. "Pull over there," she said, pointing at the area she'd spied. Duward did as she asked, bumping into a hill. He was great at driving, but hadn't had much practice at landing.

She laughed. "Guess I was too focused on teaching you the go part and not the stop part."

They climbed out and cautiously made their way toward the area that seemed to be some sort of crevice.

"It's close enough to Kidal that Andro could have made it here. And look," she said, pointing at the ground, "footprints."

The angels and Allie drew their swords as they approached the crevice.

"I do not sense an evil presence," Metatron murmured. "But I with the tricks the demons have played upon us, I do not doubt they could have some sort of masking power."

Allie nodded. "They are sneaky buggers, that's for sure."

Zad snorted a laugh at her comment. "Yeah, they're using a lot of powers that we haven't seen before. Don't know how they got their abilities, but it's hard to trust anything we've learned about them over all the previous millennia."

The crevice turned out to be a narrow cave that extended deep within the hill.

"I think it's an old mine shaft," Duward murmured close to Allie's ear, making her jump. Since he didn't have the enhanced eyesight that she and the angels had, he was sticking close to her in the darkness.

"Why do you say that, big guy?"

His big hand groped for her arm, then slid down to her hand, lifting it to the cave's wall. "Rough stone. This has been cut, not a natural formation."

Allie was surprised by that. Duward was really smart. Brave, too. She was glad to have him on her side.

But it seemed a bit... *odd*, that he'd just appeared to save her and Alejandro. It was also weird that he was so much bigger than any other human she'd come across in a thousand years.

Considering how deceitful the demons were since The Releasing, everything about Duward was a bit suspicious. She didn't like distrusting her new friend, but she couldn't help it, not after all the things she'd gone through in the past year.

Like that saying from the Old Age, if it seems too good to be true, it probably is, she sighed to herself and made a mental note to ask Metatron to see if he could sense anything unusual about the guy since her own abilities were hogtied.

The cave was narrow, but very long. At least the ceiling was tall enough that the angels didn't have to stoop in their present form.

Allie wanted to call out to Alejandro, but if someone — or something — else was in there, she didn't want to alert them. Wild animals weren't a worry in the New Age, but demons definitely were.

Instead of calling out, she focused on listening for any sounds in the darkness ahead.

It was getting darker with each step they took as they moved farther into the hill. Even she was starting to have trouble seeing and stumbled a few times, which caused Duward to fall into her.

After they nearly crashed to the cave floor, Metatron sighed and suddenly the cave was filled with a pale red glow. Allie glanced over her shoulder to see that the angel himself was glowing.

"Christmas is saved thanks to you, Rudolph," she whispered. Duward snickered at that, which startled her. If he got the joke, that meant maybe there was one person in the New Age who would understand her humor. She would have to ask him after they got out of the cave.

They walked a little farther when a slight shuffling noise drew her attention. She sensed the angels tensing behind them and knew they'd heard it too.

Thanks to Metatron's glow, Allie could see a shelf of sorts in the wall ahead of them. Running down the wall under that shelf was a thin stripe of some liquid substance.

Blood.

Allie rushed forward and tried to see if Alejandro was on the shelf, but it was too high for her. Metatron moved up behind her and peered over her head.

"He's here." The angel then reached into the dark area of the shelf and carefully pulled Alejandro out, cradling him like a small child.

He was injured. Badly. He was covered in blood and unconscious. Allie couldn't tell where he was wounded though, and her brow furrowed in worry. It didn't look like her friend had much time left. She looked up at Metatron.

"Can you transfer him back to the contrans?" She looked at Zad. "And can you take Duward? He can heal Andro."

All three males scowled at her. "What about you?" Duward asked.

"I'll come back to transfer her," Zad offered. Allie gave him a look as she held up the chain.

"You can't, remember? This stupid thing stops me from transferring, even if someone else is doing it." She waved her hand dismissively.

"I'll be fine. It's not like there's something in this cave that's gonna grab me. Besides," she added as she jerked her thumb over her shoulder at her sword, "it's not like I'm helpless."

Zad leaned down and grabbed her chain. His eyebrow cocked, the unspoken meaning all too clear. Allie felt her face heat and hoped the blush wasn't obvious in Metatron's red glow.

"I'll be careful this time," she grumbled.

"Yeah," Zad drawled, "try not to get a matching bracelet slapped on the other wrist."

"Jerk," Allie muttered as she punched him in the arm while he laughed. She could swear Duward's eyes about bugged out of his head again. *He probably thinks the angel is going to smite me or something,* she laughed to herself.

"Go on, get outta here," she told them as she pretended to kick Zad in the butt.

And in just a moment, they did. She felt for the wall to start making her way back out of the cave, she shuddered at the sudden darkness.

It was too much like The Pit for her liking.

Chapter 10

BY THE TIME she finally makes it far enough along that the cave wasn't pitch black, Allie was mentally and emotionally exhausted. The dark reminded her too much of The Pit... and that was definitely a place she'd rather forget.

She thought the guys would have come back to her after they healed Alejandro. She wasn't sure how much time had passed while she slowly groped her way along the cave passages, but it was surely long enough for them to have finished the job and transferred back to her.

"Quit being a baby," Allie grumbled to herself. "You're the freaking Mistress. Warriors don't need an escort. The guys are probably doing some male bonding or something. Or maybe Andro's witnessing to Duward. Obviously more important than holding your hand."

She didn't want to admit that her feelings were hurt.

When the light was finally dim enough that she could see where she was going, she ran. The chain was a pain, whacking her in the back of the legs as she ran and wrapping around her at times, tripping her.

Frustrated, she finally stopped and held her arm

out to the side, then wrapped the chain around her waist like a belt. When she put her arm back down, the slack made a long loop that hit her at the side of her calf and she knew she'd be bruised up and down the leg from having it slam against her as she ran, but at least it wouldn't trip her.

It took a minute for her eyes to adjust to the light once she exited the cave. The contrans was where they'd left it, but the guys were nowhere to be seen. Allie frowned at that; there was no way they'd leave her, she reassured herself. And it wasn't like they'd been captured, not with Zad and Metatron there.

But where are they? Allie wondered if the angels had transferred back to the part of the cave where they'd found Alejandro and they'd missed each other. She shook that thought away; they wouldn't have done that. Instead, they would have transferred right to her since they knew she was going to head toward the cave's entrance.

When she reached the contrans, she saw the healing rod on the floor in the back. There was blood all over the seat, which meant they had made it to the vehicle at least. And it looked like Duward had used the rod, so hopefully Alejandro had been healed.

She sighed and planted her hands on her hips as she looked around. Even though she was standing at the base of the hill, she was still higher than most of the terrain and could see for a long way.

Other than Kidal in the distance, there was no

sign of anyone. Or anything.

Allie closed her eyes and tried to open her senses, even though she knew it wouldn't work with the shackle attached. Still, it was worth a try.

Nothing.

She sighed and looked around at the ground. There were a lot of footprints, but that didn't tell her anything. The angels had huge feet — she often called Zad "Sasquatch" — and their prints were easiest to spot. Duward had big feet too and she saw his prints. There were some smaller prints that she assumed had to be Alejandro's, which was a good sign if he had been walking.

But there seemed to be a lot of prints. Much more than two men and two angels would make. The dirt was scuffed in places, too, like the guys had slid.

Or maybe they'd been dragged.

Her heartrate sped up as she looked more closely at the ground. There were definitely more prints than four guys would have made. *Unless they were dancing...* Despite her worry, Allie grinned at the mental image from that thought.

Her grin turned to snickers when she pictured Metatron and Duward two-stepping. Alejandro and Zad salsa dancing. The picture was just too much and she leaned against the contrans, giggling. She couldn't even bring herself to worry about someone hearing her as she laughed harder and harder, shaking the contrans.

"Ugh, get a grip, girl!" she chastised herself as more giggles escaped. She knew she was probably getting hysterical, which was not surprising. But it was embarrassing, even if no one was around to see it.

She cleared her throat and forced herself to concentrate as a giggle escaped every few seconds. The prints headed off toward Kidal, which meant that someone had somehow managed to overtake the angels. That idea was sobering enough that her laughter left completely.

Allie frowned at the city in the distance. She didn't think it was possible to capture warrior angels. Unless... *they were shackled with Pit chains.* She looked at her wrist, remembering Duward saying that there had been many others like the one attached to her created.

But that would mean that someone had managed to sneak up on the guys, which was pretty much impossible, especially with Metatron always using his senses. It was the one thing he always harped on.

Which meant that someone had to have transferring abilities.

She thought back to Kidal and how she'd been shocked to find herself shackled by the demon, who she was sure hadn't been behind her before then. But demons didn't have the ability to transfer.

Did they?

Allie groaned at the thought. Lucifer had the ability; maybe he'd figured out a way to share his powers with his minions. That made sense, because they'd seen a lot of weird stuff since The Releasing, demons doing things that they shouldn't have been able to do.

She was going to have to assume that the angels had been shackled and captured. Along with Duward and Alejandro. Again. Poor guy had been captured more times than she had, and that was saying a lot.

The problem was that Allie had no idea what to do about rescuing her friends. It wasn't like she could go storming into Kidal and make a stand against the thousands of Abba's enemies living there. Especially not with the stupid shackle.

She needed help.

Allie released the lock on the contrans and climbed inside, then reengaged the lock. No one could get to her with it engaged, so she relaxed and moved into the spirit.

Of course, she first sought out Abba. But for some reason, she couldn't access Him. No matter how hard she tried, it was like there was a barrier blocking her from getting to Him.

That caused her to panic, even more than when she'd been captured by the demon and paralyzed, then hung in The Pit for what felt like decades, or the time she'd awakened to find herself in Lucifer's bedroom.

Having no access to her Father was terrifying.

And unexplainable. There was no reason that she could think of that she shouldn't be able to reach Him...

Unless...

She moaned when she wondered if the shackle was preventing her from having contact with Him. Since it was designed by evil beings with evil in mind, with it attached to her she might not be able to enter into Abba's presence, not even in the spirit.

Okay, don't panic. She shoved aside the horrid feeling of separation and instead focused on her husband. Nick would at least be able to go to Abba and tell Him what happened.

She was blocked from Nick too. Now she was panicking for real.

Allie then tried to access anyone she could think of, even though Metatron had told her that the spirit world worked like transferring — you could only contact those you were closest to. Which for her meant Abba, Nick, Zad and Metatron. But that didn't stop her from trying to reach Robin, Justin, and any other Remnant she'd been somewhat close to. She tried the angels too.

But nothing.

Sighing in defeat, she left the spirit world, then glared at the shackle on her wrist. She had no doubt that the stupid thing was keeping her from contacting her loved ones. But then she remembered that she'd been able to reach Zad and Metatron before, so what was different?

Maybe it's the place.

When she'd reached Zad and Metatron before, they'd been on Shadar. Since the shackle had been created on Earth, maybe it had a limitation.

Entering the spirit world again, she tried to go to Shadar, but nothing happened. Another groan of frustration left her as she suddenly felt stupid. The spirit world was tied to spirits, not places. *Duh.*

She then tried to find her angel friends. If she'd been able to contact them before, then she should be able to now... but, again, nothing.

Fighting down the terror she was starting to feel at being so isolated from everyone, started the contrans and then proceeded to race back across the Inner Circle toward The City.

She'd just have to contact them the old-fashioned way.

Chapter 11

I T TOOK TWO days to get back to the Paradise Gardens, and another hour to realize that not only was she unable to access anyone in the spirit or by transferring, she also couldn't enter the Gardens.

Which meant she couldn't enter The City either.

She'd done a lot of thinking as she'd traveled, reasoning that all her problems centered on the stupid satanic bracelet she was wearing. And her fears were manifested when she realized she couldn't get anywhere near the good people. Since the danged thing was created by evil, and the Gardens and City were sin-free, the evil couldn't enter.

Short of cutting off her sword arm, she was stuck.

Allie sat on the hood of the contrans where she'd parked just outside of the Gardens, scowling. She'd tried to get inside through several different places, but it was like an invisible barrier was preventing it. She'd also tried yelling, calling out for help and even throwing rocks into the greenery, but no one had responded.

It occurred to her then that she could try the Remnant mansion. It was on the edge of the Inner Circle, so there shouldn't be anything preventing her from going there. Then maybe she could find someone who could take a message to Abba for her.

Hopefully Nick was there. She sure could use some comfort from her husband.

The sun was low in the sky by the time she pulled the contrans up to the front door of the mansion and stared at the windows. It was still early enough that people should be moving about, but the place looked deserted.

Instead of panicking again, Allie reminded herself that they were probably all still on Shadar. The planet had much longer days than Earth, which allowed for long days of practicing. It could be hours before anyone returned.

She sighed heavily and ran a weary hand over her face. "Oh well," she muttered, "might as well find something to eat and get a shower while I can."

~~

After finding some bread and melon in the kitchen, Allie went upstairs to the apartment she shared with Nick and her angel friends. She was aching for a hot shower, especially since she'd only been able to take an occasional cold bath for the last month.

Showering with the chain was an adventure. It kept banging her body whenever she'd raise her hands to wash herself, to the point the shower wasn't even enjoyable and she hurried to finish.

Once dressed in new undergarments, she pulled her cumbersome uniform back on. Abba had wanted it to draw attention; with all the gold and silver adornment, it certainly did that. It was also tiring to wear; with all the extra weight she was dragging around, Allie figured she was getting a heck of a workout just walking around.

After she was fully dressed, Allie tried once more to find Nick in the spirit, but again, it was like no one was there.

So weird.

As far as she could tell, the mansion was completely empty. She knew the Remnants would be out training, and Serene, their Healer, would be with them to deal with the numerous injuries that always occurred with practice.

Abba had given them other staff — cooks, cleaners, et cetera — but she didn't see any of them either. Coupled with the inability to find anyone through the spiritual realm, Allie was starting to feel abandoned.

And very alone.

She sighed. Moping about wasn't going to solve any problems, that was for sure and she thought maybe getting some sun and fresh air would help, so she went out to the garden behind the mansion.

It was a beautiful day, even though it was growing late. She wandered through the garden, remembering the other times she'd visited. It was her favorite place to be, next to Abba's presence. It was there that she'd married Nick, where Abba had comforted her, and where her bobcat friend loved to lounge.

As if conjuring her by thought, Allie spied the cat stretched out in the greenery beside the path she'd been strolling down.

"Charo!" Allie squealed in delight. It had been months since she'd seen her friend. The cat's tail twitched, then she lazily lifted her head as Allie pushed through the shrubbery. She collapsed to her knees beside the cat and wrapped her arms around her neck.

The cat purred softly in response. "I'm so glad to see you," Allie murmured into her neck as her eyes filled with tears. She was so thankful to have someone there, even if it was an animal who couldn't talk back.

"Where are the others? On Shadar? And how was Serariel? You were gone a long time. I was worried about you." Even though she knew the cat couldn't talk back, it didn't stop Allie from having a one-sided conversation.

That was the big question on her mind — how Serariel was. She still had a lot of guilt over his sacrifice for her.

In response to her questions, Charo rolled onto her back for a belly rub. Allie laughed and obliged. She scratched her friend and petted her, then sat back and sighed.

"I have another favor to ask you," she said and laughed again when Charo opened one eye and gave her a look.

"I'm sorry, but you're the only one who can help me. It's super important and since no one is here and I can't transfer—" she held up the shackle to show the cat, "—it's up to you to save the day. But this time, you don't have to walk half-way across the world. I'll drive."

~~

It was long past midnight by the time they arrived at the Paradise Gardens. Allie knew that most people would be asleep, so she asked Charo to go straight to the Inner Sanctuary and seek out Abba. Even though the cat couldn't speak, Abba would of course be able to understand her.

"Tell Him that Zad and Metatron, as well as Alejandro and my new friend Duward, have been captured and that I think they're in Kidal." Charo turned and tensed to jump out.

"Wait," Allie said, stopping her, "tell Him too about my shackle and chain, that they're from The Pit and how I'm stuck not being able to do much."

Charo nodded, then hopped out of the contrans and started trotting off. Allie frowned.

"Hold on!" she called. Charo stopped and looked over her shoulder. "Can you just ask Him to come here and I'll explain it all to Him?"

Allie laughed when the cat rolled her eyes and continued on her trek.

It was quite a while before Abba suddenly

appeared before her. Allie leapt off the contrans hood and started to run toward Him for a hug, but He held His hand up to stop her. She froze in her tracks, mouth hanging open. Abba had never denied her His affection before, and Allie felt her world crashing in around her.

What have I done? She wondered as her whole body started shaking in fear at the thought of Abba's denial of her.

Abba gave her a chiding look. "You haven't done anything, daughter." He gestured at her arm where the chain hung. "With that thing on you, I can't touch you. And for that, I am truly sorry."

Relief flooded through her, while at the same time she cursed Lucifer once more. If she saw him again, she was going to wear his head as a hat like he'd threatened to do to her. Abba laughed.

"Now *that's* a picture," He chuckled, reading her mind. "But please tell Me why you're here. Charo wouldn't tell Me and in fact, was more interested in eating the cheese off Paul's plate."

Allie laughed, while cringing at the thought of the lecture she was going to get from the apostle the next time she saw him. Paul gave epic lectures, which could turn into real snoozefests. She always said she needed to pack a lunch because he was so long-winded.

Which usually led to another lecture about her sassiness.

"Well, as You already know, I got shackled again. But You also know it's not one that You created." She held up her wrist and scowled at the thing.

"Apparently, it was created by Lucifer from the same material as The Pit chains. It was a demon who put it on me."

Abba's eyebrow rose. "And did I not tell you to watch your back, child?"

Allie felt a blush creep up her neck. "Yeah, well I was also trying to watch over Alejandro, which isn't easy, let me tell You. He starts testifying and he gets totally reckless. And there was the fact that we were in Kidal, which is totally antagonistic. Like the whole city. There was only one guy who helped me."

Abba nodded. "Duward, yes I know. He is going to be one of Mine."

Allie grinned at that. She was so glad to know that her new friend would be with her for eternity.

"Oh, and apparently Lucifer has been stockpiling firearms and ammunition. Duward showed me an armory." Her grin returned.

"We stole a bunch of his weapons." Abba laughed again.

"You know stealing is a sin, but in this case we'll call it 'enemy spoils'. And I will be addressing the angels' insubordination, by the way. It is a just punishment that they have been captured. I am sure their egos have taken a major blow."

Allie felt the need to defend her friends, even though they *were* in the wrong. She'd warned them not to stay with her, but they were stubborn jerks.

"Yes, they are," Abba agreed, before sighing and glancing off in the distance. Allie was mesmerized by the way the reflection of the stars made His eyes shimmer even more than normal.

"I suppose I need to be lenient with them, considering they're so close to you."

Allie felt relief at that. "And don't forget that You assigned them to me as bodyguards, so technically they were just obeying Your original command," she reminded Him.

Abba threw His head back and laughed. Allie chuckled with Him. He then looked at her. "I always miss you when you're gone," He grinned. "And I will allow that you're correct... to a point," He chuckled.

"So, what will You do?" Allie asked. She couldn't wait to hear what Abba was going to do to help her friends. Fire and brimstone? Hailstones the size of baby elephants? A city-swallowing earthquake?

He grinned at her thoughts. "Nothing."

Allie felt her eyes bugging. "Nothing? But—" Abba held His hand up to silence her arguments.

"I'm not going to do anything. That is up to you. I will say that after this, you need to go straight to Lucifer's army. Don't stop at any more towns and villages. They will no longer hear Alejandro's message of My salvation. You will go directly to Lucifer's army.

Many there will hear the message, have no doubt."

Abba sighed and started to put His hand on Allie's shoulder, but made a fist and pulled back, regret crossing His face.

"For now, all I can do is tell you where the angels and Alejandro are being held. Releasing them is up to you and your abilities." He gave her a stern look.

"You need to quit doubting those abilities, daughter. I have graced you with much talent and craftiness. You have trained for a thousand years with the Remnants and have been a most excellent leader to them. Now is the time to put those talents to good use."

Chapter 12

BBA ALLOWED CHARO to go with her. And while she would have loved having other Remnants with her, especially Nick, Allie was thankful for her cat friend's presence. If Abba wouldn't help her, at least she had a bobcat with lethal teeth and claws on her side.

She glanced at her passenger. *Maybe not so lethal,* she thought as Charo snored softly next to her, her drool running down the contrans seat.

Abba may not have wanted to help her with reinforcements, but He did give her a map of where she'd be able to find her friends. He also gave her a set of her own shackles to use on a demon. She hoped she could capture one and make him take the shackle off her wrist.

Her friends were being held in a cave far inside the mountain opposite of where they'd found Alejandro. Apparently, there was a huge mine system in the mountain that she hadn't been aware of. Probably what Duward had been talking about, left over from the Old Age.

The entrance was hidden behind a rock outcropping, but thanks to Abba's perfect map, Allie found it easily. She'd barely gotten the contrans stopped when Charo leapt out and trotted toward the entrance.

"Hold up," Allie told her, keeping her voice low. Abba had warned her again to "watch her back," and told her that there would be guards in the cave.

The cat stopped and looked back at her as Allie armed herself with her sword. She then grabbed the healing rod and tucked it into her belt. Hopefully, Duward was alright and would be able to heal anyone who needed it.

She then stepped up to Charo and put her hand on her head. "We need to be very careful here. Abba said there were guards watching over our friends."

Charo looked back into the cave entrance and put her nose in the air, sniffing. She then looked at Allie and nodded.

The familiar musky odor of damp earth filled her nostrils as they made their way into the cave. Allie and Charo hugged the wall as they cautiously moved deeper into the cavern, not because of the darkness, but to keep as "invisible" as possible.

A murmur of voices stopped them in their tracks once they were deep into the cave. It should have been very dark at that point, Allie thought, but there was a light source ahead and it looked like there were numerous caves branching out from the tunnel. The perfect place for jail cells.

More than anything, she wished she could reach out to her friends and let them know to be aware of her presence, to tell them she was there and would release them soon. Hopefully. Not being able to converse with them was annoying, to say the least.

She moved close to the first cave and peered in, trying to see if it was occupied, but it was too dark.

Charo softly growled and that made Allie pause. She glanced back at the cat to see that her hackles were up as she stared down the tunnel. She was crouching, ready to leap at any moment. Allie turned to see what had caught her attention.

A man that Allie was sure was a demon had moved into the tunnel and was looking their way. She could tell he couldn't see them though. It was pitch black behind them and they weren't close enough to the light to be seen. She didn't know if demons had enhanced eyesight like she and Charo did, but she sure hoped not.

The demon must have decided there wasn't any threat, as he turned and moved to the entrance of one of the caves. He stood in the tunnel and looked in.

"You are not so mighty now, are you Zadkiel?" the demon taunted. "Nor you, Celestial Scribe." Allie heard the sound of rattling chains in response to the taunts.

The demon laughed. "Don't bother. The shackles can't be broken, even by the Heavenly Host."

Allie's fists clenched and more than anything, she wanted to run down the tunnel and wrap her own chain around the demon's stinking neck.

How dare he tease the angels? *That's my job!*

"At least we know where one of them is," she

whispered to Charo, so low that only the cat would be able to hear her. The demon moved on to the next cave and did the same taunting of the inhabitant. From what Allie gathered from his end of the conversation, it was Alejandro.

So that just left figuring out where Duward was.

A slight suspicion entered her mind then about Duward, if he was really on their side, or if he had been involved in the capture of Alejandro and the angels. But then she remembered her talk with Abba, and she set those worries aside. Even if Duward had betrayed them, he would eventually be turned to the good side.

Once the demon moved away, Allie and Charo crept to the first cave. It had what looked like iron bars on the front, making it look like a jail cell. It was too dark to see much, although she could make out two bodies that seemed to be shackled to the wall like the other cell's occupant had been. She glanced around to make sure there weren't any more demons in the area.

"Zad!" she hissed. A low moan greeted her. Not a good sign.

"Metatron?" she whispered, but there was no answer from him, not even a moan. She tried the door, but of course it was locked.

"We need keys," she said, thinking out loud. Charo must have decided Allie was giving her a mission because she trotted off in the direction the demon had gone.

Allie rolled her eyes, but she figured if anyone had a chance at stealing keys, it was Charo. She knew from experience that the cat was sneaky.

The next cell had a light outside of it, casting a dim glow on the interior. She could see who she assumed was Alejandro lying on a cot. Surprisingly, he wasn't shackled. In fact, he had been given a blanket. But he looked to be in bad shape, and she wondered if his injuries were from before, or if these were new.

Poor guy.

She turned then and examined the rest of the area. There were more cells farther down in the deep cavern and she could hear small noises, shuffling, murmurs, and what sounded like someone scratching.

Charo was nowhere to be seen, so Allie carefully pulled her sword out. She regretted not bringing her shield too, but not only was it cumbersome, it was also very flashy. If her uniform and sword didn't reflect the light and give her position away, the shield definitely would have.

She crept up on the next cell and peered in. The door wasn't latched and the cell was empty, so she moved to the next one. That door was closed, but it was too dark to see inside. She had to assume that if it was locked, there was an occupant. Hopefully it was Duward.

The creak of metal hinges drew her attention further into the dark cavern and she froze in place.

She squinted; even with her excellent eyesight, it was too dark to see clearly. But she could make out movement, too close to the ground to be a human.

Go get 'em, girl, Allie mentally cheered her cat friend on.

Charo slid into an open cell which must have been was empty, because she immediately came out and moved into the next cell that had a soft light glowing within. When she didn't come back out right away, Allie held her breath and started moving closer in case her friend needed help.

A startled voice cried out, the words unintelligible. It sounded garbled, like maybe the speaker was being strangled.

Or having its throat ripped out.

In a few moments, Charo came trotting back out of the cave with a ring of keys in her mouth. Her bloody mouth. She spotted Allie and sprinted toward her. Allie grinned.

"Good girl," she mouthed then cocked her head to indicate returning to the other cells. They stopped first at the cell where she hoped Duward would be and spent way too long trying to find the right key. Once they finally got it open, Allie was saddened to see that occupant was dead, but thankfully it wasn't her large friend. The body that was hanging by frail wrists shackled to the stone wall was a normal-sized human. Or had been at one time.

Allie shuddered at the gruesome sight.

They checked the tunnel first, then crept to a cell and Allie was relieved to see Alejandro, even though he was in even worse shape than she'd thought. It took a minute to find the correct key again and Allie was gritting her teeth by the time they finally got the door open. The hinges creaked slightly, and she cringed.

He didn't move. Allie moved closer and nudged his shoulder. "Andro," she whispered near his ear. "It's Allie. Are you okay?"

Her friend didn't make a sound, and that was really worrisome. She grimaced and glanced down at Charo.

"We need to find Duward first," she whispered to the yellow-eyed cat. "He can heal the guys so we can get out of here. It's not like either one of us can carry them."

Charo purred in agreement, then she sat and looked at Allie. "What?" Of course, the cat didn't answer, but she gave her a droll look. A dim lightbulb went off in Allie's brain.

"Oh, right. You have no idea who Duward is." Charo gave her a look that said she questioned Allie's intelligence and she huffed out a quiet laugh.

She thought about letting the cat smell her to get Duward's scent, but she'd showered. But then she wondered if her uniform might still have his scent from where he'd carried her. She turned her back to the cat and squatted down.

"He carried me for a long time, so my back might smell like him," she whispered. "See if you can get his scent. He's a big guy, almost as big as the angels in their human form. He's very dark too. Darker than even the apostles."

Allie could hear the cat sniffing her, then nothing. She glanced over her shoulder, but Charo was gone. Allie laughed to herself. She was certainly efficient.

Since there wasn't anything she could do for Alejandro at the moment, she left the cell and pulled the door closed behind her without latching it. Then she moved to the next cell where the angels were and fumbled through the keys until she found the right one, then unlocked their door too.

Charo had been gone for a while and Allie was starting to get worried. She leaned against the wall and crossed her arms over her chest, then bent her leg and propped her foot against the wall. It was a very casual stance for someone who was stressed in every sense of the word.

There more noises coming from farther away, but Allie didn't care about them, not unless she heard "Oh look, there's a cat! We should smash it with a rock," or something like that. But she knew Charo was very cautious and stealthy. It was unlikely she would be caught, or even spotted.

Hopefully.

After a few more long moments that were making Allie twitch, Charo came back. The cat stopped in front of her and jerked her head down the hall, obviously wanting Allie to follow.

Charo led her to a tunnel she hadn't seen before. It was even darker there and she had to rely on the cat for direction, since she obviously knew where she was going. Allie just hoped the weren't any low ceilings to knock herself out on.

She bumped into the back of her feline friend when she suddenly stopped. Allie felt along the stone wall to the side and then down the bars of what was obviously another cell door. She then fumbled along the bars until she found the keyhole.

"This is gonna be seriously difficult," she whispered to the cat. "Not only can I not see the keyhole, but I won't be able to tell which key I've already tried. We could be here for days," she grumbled.

A very deep voice startled her then, making her drop the keys.

"The door is not locked."

Chapter 13

D UWARD, YOU SCARED the crap outta me!" Allie squeaked to her friend, who reached through the cell bars and placed his big hands over hers.

He chuckled. "Sorry, little warrior," he murmured as she pulled her hands from his and bent to feel around for the dropped keys. It took a few moments, but her fingers finally touched metal and she snatched them up. Since all the cell doors were unlocked now, she probably wouldn't need them, but figured she should hang on to them, just in case.

Allie's life had been a series of those "just in case" moments.

The cell door creaked, and Allie hurried to get out of the way, bumping into Charo again and stepping on her foot. The cat hissed at her and Allie muttered, "Sorry."

In a flash, she was wrapped up in Duward's big arms. "Are you hurt?" he mumbled in her ear.

Allie shook her head. "I'm fine," she whispered. "Are *you* okay?" He released her and she stepped back. It was weird, talking to someone but not being able to see them.

"A few injuries, but nothing to speak of."

Allie frowned then. "Why was your cell

unlocked?" It was another oddity, and something else that made her doubt Duward's honesty. *He'll be Abba's soon,* she reminded herself again.

She sensed him shrug. "I picked the lock."

Allie breathed a quiet laugh. "Jack of all trades," she teased. "So why didn't you leave?"

"I just picked it a little bit ago and then I heard voices, so I was waiting for the opportunity. We need to get back to the vehicle and get the healing rod. I'm afraid your angel friends are badly injured."

Allie nodded, even though he couldn't see it. "Yeah, I figured that. I know where they're being held though. And I have the healing rod, so you can fix them and Andro up and we can get out of here."

Duward grunted. "The angels are likely chained with the same shackles you wear."

Allie grinned. "Then let's catch us a demon."

~~

Allie and Duward made a plan of attack using Charo as a distraction. She hoped that the demons would be confused by the cat's presence and wouldn't attack her.

At least, that's what she prayed to Abba to have happen.

She and Duward waited until they heard a commotion in the far tunnels, then watched from their darkened hiding place as a lone demon hurried toward them. Allie nudged Duward with her elbow and motioned with her head to follow her.

The demon was concentrating on getting to the source of the commotion and didn't even notice when she stepped out and clotheslined him. The movement sent the chain from her shackle swinging out and back around. Allie ducked just in time to avoid being hit and hoped Duward didn't get smacked too.

The chain finished wrapping itself around the demon's neck before his knees buckled and he went down. Of course, that meant Allie went with him since she was now attached to him.

They both "oofed" at the impact and then she was staring into the startled eyes of the handsome demon. Allie batted her eyes at him and smiled shyly.

"Why, I always wanted to catch me a man," she cooed quietly in an exaggerated southern drawl. "Shoulda thought of the chain sooner!"

She heard Duward snicker behind her as she put her hand over the demon's mouth before he recovered and yelled for help.

"Get the shackles from the back of my belt," she told Duward and felt a tug on her belt as he did so.

He attached them to the demon's wrists, then unwound the chain while Allie still held her hand over the demon's mouth. She jumped when she felt a tongue against her palm, and she narrowed her eyes at him. She could swear the demon was smiling at her.

Well, I can play that game too, jerkwad. Allie leaned forward and kissed his nose, almost laughing as his gray eyes widened in shock.

"Well, it's been fun, but I just no longer feel the same way about you," she said sassily as she pushed to a sitting position on the demon's stomach.

"It's not you, though," she sighed. "It's me." The demon rolled his eyes at her and she chuckled.

Duward then handed her a strip of cloth then and she glanced at her friend in question. She had no idea where he got it from, but since it was a demon they were dealing with, she didn't care if it was the rag they used to cleaned the latrine.

"Rip off a fist-sized piece, would you?" she asked Duward. He did so, then handed it to her, she then waggled her finger from her free hand in the demon's face.

"Don't make a sound when I take my hand away, or else I'm gonna cut off your dangly bits with the knife I use to clean mud and poop from the soles of my boots, got it?"

Her lips twitched when the demon's eyes widened even further, and he nodded quickly. Demons definitely liked their dangly bits.

After she stuffed the bunched-up rag in his mouth, she tied what was left of the strip around his head and then Duward yanked the demon off the ground. Once again, Allie was surprised at the guy's strength.

They led the demon down the dark tunnel toward the angels' cell. Allie wanted to get the shackle off her wrist, but she wanted her friends healed and released first.

In the tunnel while she and Duward had waited for Charo to make her distraction, she'd thought about who should be the first to be healed. While Alejandro was probably the most injured and suffering more than the angels who had immortality on their side, Allie felt it was smarter to heal the angels and then the Chief Witness. She knew they'd need the angels if the demons realized that the strange appearance of a bobcat in their cavern was meant to draw their attention away from the prisoners.

"Are there any torches down here?" she murmured to the demon. He glanced at her and nodded then raised his shackled hand to point toward a doorless cell. Allie winced when his chain rattled, but whatever Charo was doing down in the deeper part of the cavern was still causing a lot of commotion.

Duward moved to the cell the demon pointed out while Allie waited in the tunnel. It was a few moments before she saw light and Duward emerged, carrying an actual flaming torch. Allie snickered.

"I meant 'torch', as in handheld battery-operated device, otherwise known as a flashlight." She shrugged. "But hey, old school is good too. Just don't catch my hair on fire."

The angels' cell door creaked when they opened it, but Allie didn't worry about the sound this time. There was too much crashing and yelling going on in the distance and she grinned. *Good girl,* she thought. She was going to have to ask Abba to reward Charo.

Duward's stomach growled then, loud enough to rival Charo's distraction. They chuckled, even the demon.

"We'll find a pic-a-nic basket when we're done, Yogi," she murmured as she patted him on the back. Surprisingly, Duward laughed, once again getting her Old Age reference.

She was going to have to ask him about that. As far as she knew, everyone who'd come through the Tribulation in the Old Age had moved to The City or the Gardens. It was their generations of offspring who'd chosen to move away from Abba.

Under the light of the torch, the angels' injuries made Allie suck in a breath. "What did they do to you," she breathed. It wasn't a question; it seemed that the demons tried to kill the angels.

Metatron looked the worst. He was bloody and it looked like there wasn't a single spot on his beautiful face that wasn't bruised. Her teeth cracked under the pressure she put on them in the effort to hold back a scream. Or tears.

The demons were going to pay.

"Vengeance is Mine."

Abba's voice filled her head then, and Allie's shoulders slumped. That wasn't what she wanted to hear; she wanted to pound the demons just as hard as they'd pounded her friends while they'd been helpless with the stupid shackles.

"But in this case, I'll make an exception. Have at 'em, daughter."

Startled by His words, Allie laughed. Duward glanced at her with an expression that said he doubted her sanity, understandably, since they were staring at her bloodied friends.

"Sorry," she muttered as she waved her hand. He shook his head at her; he probably thought she was hysterical. *As if.* Warriors didn't get hysterical. They got even.

Duward then held out the torch for her to take and she pulled the healing rod from her belt and handed it to him. She wanted her friends healed before they jostled them by removing the chains.

"This is going to take a while," Duward muttered. Allie nodded; that was an understatement.

She grew tired after what seemed like an hour of Duward's healing efforts, but she knew it was probably only minutes. She dragged the demon by his chain toward the wall so she could lean against it, yet still keep him close. He leaned against the wall with her and watched Duward.

Allie had always thought it was kind of weird how the demons weren't always truly evil. *Well, yeah, they are,* she corrected herself. But often, they showed a more human side that always threw her off balance. She didn't like that feeling. She wanted to keep the knowledge that they were the enemy in mind at all times.

Duward had started with Metatron since he seemed the worst off. Allie noted that he started with the big angel's feet and worked his way up. She figured that was smart, because if he'd healed his head first and the angel woke up, he'd be in a lot of pain from the rest of the injuries.

Once he was done with Metatron's body, he moved to Zad, but he hadn't healed Metraton's head for some reason, so the angel was still unconscious. Allie frowned at that but figured Duward had his reason. Zad took much less time to heal, and Duward hadn't even gotten to his head when he came to.

"Hey kiddo," he murmured when he spotted Allie. He tried to smile, but it looked like his jaw was broken and Allie shook her head at him.

"Don't move yet," she admonished. "Wait 'til Duward is done."

Zad didn't listen, of course, and turned his head toward his companion. When he saw Metatron's face, he winced.

"Got it worse than me," he gritted out. "He fought hard though."

Allie moved closer to him, dragging the demon

with her. She didn't want him getting far enough away to think he could attempt an escape.

"How did you guys get beat up anyway?" It was something she could have asked Duward, but she wanted to hear it from the angels, since they would know exactly what had happened.

Zad sighed and closed his eyes when Duward got to his face. "They just appeared out of nowhere," he said so quietly that even Allie had to strain to hear what he was saying.

"Popped up behind us before Duward had barely started healing Andro. They snapped these shackles on us and then our powers were useless."

Zad glanced back at his sword still strapped to his back. The demons wouldn't have been able to remove it, since it was a celestial instrument. Touching it would have been suicide for them.

"Hard to fight when your hands are tied," he said with a wry look.

"Tell me about it," Allie muttered as she glanced away. "Well, we got this demon here now, so he can take those off you." She yanked the demon toward her friend and motioned to him. The demon looked at her, then glanced toward the cell door, probably looking to see if anyone was coming.

Dangly bits in danger or not, getting caught releasing the prisoners probably had a worse sentence.

It took just seconds for the demon to release the

shackles. Zad groaned as he lowered his newly freed arms. Allie could sympathize; she knew what it was like to have your extremities held in awkward positions for long periods. Duward frowned and moved the healing rod over the angel's shoulders.

When the demon released Metatron, he nearly fell over in his unconscious state and Allie had to grab him to lower him gently to the hard floor.

"Oof," she grunted, "you need to lay off Pierre's custards big guy." The angel had a huge sweet tooth and was the Remnant chef's favorite taste tester. She then held out her wrist and the demon removed her shackle, wincing as she rubbed her sore joint.

Never again, she promised herself. She'd rather cut off her own hand than have a Lucifer-created shackle on her again.

Once Zad was healed and on his feet, Duward moved back to Metatron. "He's going to take a lot longer," he said, stating the obvious. The angel was barely recognizable.

Allie had avoided looking at her friend too closely, but now it couldn't be helped. It looked like most of the bones in his face had been broken. She knew Duward had healed a broken leg and probably some internal injuries too.

There was no reason for the demons to have beaten the angels. Once they were cuffed with the shackles, they were pretty much at their captors' mercy. Her earlier benevolent thoughts of the demons fled and she ground her already abused teeth.

With a growl, she turned and grabbed the demon's chain and yanked him to the far dark corner where she chained his wrists to the rings embedded on the wall. She pulled on them to make sure he was secure and then she pulled a knife from her belt and moved to Duward, placing it on the ground next to him. She glanced back at the demon to make sure he was paying attention.

"If he tries anything, cut off his privates."

Duward turned and stared at her with wide eyes, then nodded slowly as he swallowed. Allie laughed; males did not like hearing about attacks on genitalia.

Allie looked at Zad. "Wanna go get some revenge?" she asked with a crooked grin. Zad grinned back but shook his head with a sigh.

"Love to, but we're already on Abba's list. He's not big on seeking vengeance."

Allie patted her friend's back. "He already gave me the go ahead," she laughed.

Zad's eyes widened. "Well, in that case, heck yeah!"

Chapter 14

WHATEVER THE commotion was that Charo started seemed to have abated by the time Allie and Zad came to the branch of the tunnel that led to the big cavern. They paused and Allie peeked around the corner.

She didn't see anything. Or anybody.

Allie looked back at Zad and shrugged with her hands out. She then pulled her sword from the scabbard and nodded toward the cavern.

Being extra careful to be as quiet as possible, they crept into the cavern and slid along the wall, which was surprisingly smooth in that area. Ahead, Allie could see more cutouts in the walls and wondered if they were more cells, just rooms or more tunnels. The place was huge.

A soft noise drew their attention to one of the nearby cutouts and they moved toward it. Allie peeked into what looked like a small cave. There were two demons inside, which wasn't surprising, but what caused Allie and Zad to chuckle was the fact that the bloodied demons were piled on top of each other.

And Charo was perched at the top like a weathervane on a barn.

"Way to go, girl," Allie whispered as she scratched the cat behind the ears. "Are there others?"

Charo gave a nod, then hopped off the bodies and walked out of the little cave, turning right.

Allie couldn't see any movement in the deep cavern. She glanced back at Zad and lifted her eyebrows in question. He shook his head slightly. Apparently, he couldn't see anyone either.

They followed Charo to the next cutout, this one a tunnel. The cat loped down the hall seemingly without a care or fear, so Allie and Zad relaxed their guard as they followed her. The tunnel had a few lights along its length and Allie could see other cutouts. Probably more tunnels.

"How far into the mountain do you think we are now?" she asked Zad. The angel shrugged.

"Probably in the middle."

"I'm guessing we're about to the back of that other cave where we found Andro," Allie told him. "Wonder if the two meet."

Zad shrugged. "Maybe—"

His words were cut off when they passed one of the cutouts and a demon horde leapt out at them. Allie didn't even have time to pull her sword when she was attacked. *Gonna be a fistfight,* she moaned to herself. She hated hand-to-hand combat. It always meant bruises and things breaking. Swords were much easier.

She saw a fist flying at her face from her

peripheral, so she ducked, then pivoted and punched the demon in the ribs. Air whooshed out of his lungs and he fell back, and another took his place. Allie kicked that one in the knee, then swung back around and swept his legs out from under him and dropped down with all her weight to elbow him in the throat.

"That's what happens when you spend your childhood watching WWE," she told the wide-eyed demon as she stood.

A blow caught her in the kidney, and she arched her back in pain before doubling over to roll out of the way, coming up to kick another demon in the chest. He flew back and hit the wall with a thud.

Zad was busy with his own group while Allie wondered where the heck Charo had run off to. After hearing a satisfying crunch when she connected with another demon's nose, she was able to step back and pull her sword out and grinned when the demons stepped back.

"Yeah, that's right, back off little girls. The odds are a little more balanced now that I have my sword, huh?" Allie taunted as she whipped an "X" in front of her body.

"Four of you to one human who trained for a thousand years on how to slice and dice demon parts. I'd say those are good odds."

Behind her, Zad chuckled as he sliced his way through his own group. Ten demons to two unarmed people — even if one of those "people" was an angel, the odds were still unfair.

Not that demons cared about fairness.

But now that they both were able to draw their swords, the demons were obviously having second thoughts. They glanced at each other, then turned tail and ran down the tunnel in the direction Charo had gone.

Allie looked at Zad and they both started chuckling at once.

And they were laughing harder just moments later when the demons started screaming like the little girls Allie had called them. Judging by the growls and snarls, the demons had met up with Charo.

"She might not be a big cat like a lion or tiger," Allie laughed, "but she makes up for it in sneakiness and snarkiness."

"And teeth and claws," Zad quipped.

They jogged down the hall to see if Charo needed any help, but laughed again when they turned a corner and saw that the cat had matters well in hand. Three demons were on the ground, whining like injured dogs as Charo cleaned her paws from their blood.

"Meeeerowwwwrrrr," the cat said, looking at them like she'd just dropped a mouse at their feet.

"Is that the last of the demons?" she asked the cat, who nodded.

"Cool," Allie said. Since all the demons in the cavern were incapacitated, they turned and headed back toward the others.

Metatron was standing outside the cell when they got back. Duward was in Alejandro's cell, still working on healing him.

"He was injured further when he was brought here," Metatron explained, arms crossed over his chest and not looking too happy. Allie assumed that was because he'd been caught unaware. The Celestial Scribe was always harping on her to "use her senses," but since he'd been caught by the enemy so easily, Allie knew it grated on him. She could have mentioned it, teased him mercilessly, but she didn't. Instead, she walked up to him and wrapped her arms around his waist, smiling when he returned the hug.

"I'm glad you're okay," she whispered against his chest. "I hated seeing you so beat up. Those stinking demon shackles suck, huh?"

A chuckle escaped the angel as his arms squeezed her. "Yes, they do," he agreed.

Duward stepped out of Alejandro's cell then, and the Chief Witness followed. Metatron released her and she stepped back, so relieved at seeing that Alejandro was all right that her eyes teared up.

"Andro," Allie breathed as she moved forward to hug her charge. It had been her duty to protect him, but she'd failed miserably. His arms tightened around her.

"I'm sorry," he breathed into her neck.

Allie shook her head. "No, it's not your fault—"

Andro squeezed her tighter. "No, it is my fault. You warned me, told me not to get too far away from you. This is totally my fault."

Allie laughed and stepped back. "Okay, maybe it's a little your fault," she quipped, grinning at him. He laughed and ran a hand over his eyes.

"Yeah, well, I'll definitely stick close to you from now on. In fact, you'll get so tired of me being under your feet that you'll be wanting to kill me yourself."

Allie rolled her eyes and punched her old friend in the shoulder. "Not likely," she grinned. She nodded toward the exit.

"You guys ready to go?" They nodded and started to head toward the exit, but a loud protest from Charo had them turning back to look at the cat.

"What girl?" Allie asked. The cat meowed again and Zad sucked in a breath. Allie glanced at him; one of the angel's gifts was animal communication.

Zad looked at Metatron and then back at Allie, his eyes wide. "She, uh, said that Serariel is here, in one of the cells."

"What?" Allie breathed as she looked back at the cat, her heart pounding. If that was the case, Allie could barely wait to find him. The angel was never far from her thoughts.

Charo meowed several more times as Zad interpreted. "She said he was never taken to The Pit, because Lucifer figured you'd try to rescue him. And that's why it took so long for her to return to the mansion, because she had to find him."

Alejandro stared at Zad. "All that from 'meow mew mew'?" Zad shrugged his shoulders.

"Okay then," Allie said as she turned back to Charo. "Please show us where he is."

Chapter 15

THEY FOUND SERARIEL in a dank, pitch black cell. The entrance was hidden behind some crates and they would have completely missed if it hadn't been for Charo. The angel had been severely injured, making Allie want to go re-kill the demons. It took Duward quite a while to patch him back together.

Once Serariel was back on his feet, they made their way out of the vast cavern system. When they passed the cell that still had the demon chained to the wall, Allie looked at Charo and told her, "Have at 'em. And head back to Abba when you're done."

They left to the sounds of garbled screams.

Since Abba had given the go-ahead to go straight to the army, they'd ditched the contrans and transferred directly to the outskirts of the enemy camp, where they surveyed the landscape from atop a hill. Allie laughed to herself; she was always observing from a hill. Unfortunately, it rarely helped. Visual reconnaissance didn't go far when you were dealing with those who specialized in falsehood.

The army had grown far larger than Allie could have imagined. Since she'd last seen it — when it had already been huge, filling acres and acres of land — it now occupied land farther than the eye could see.

The camp sort of resembled a city, with clusters of tents set up and what looked like paths in between, like city blocks. But if it *were* a city, it would be the largest one ever in the New Age.

It was... startling.

"How big do you think it is?" Alejandro breathed. Allie glanced at the Chief Witness; he looked like a kid who'd just been given the keys to a candy store and told to pick whatever he wanted. He'd be witnessing to them before they even got off the hill.

"Approximately twelve square miles, thirty-one square kilometers, three thousand one hundred eight hectares, or seven thousand six hundred eighty acres. Those numbers are, of course, rounded."

Allie gave Metatron a look. "Seriously?"

He shrugged. "As Celestial Scribe, it is my job to know such things."

Allie tilted her head. "I thought you recorded the sins and merits of humans."

He nodded. "I do, but I also—"

"Hold up," Zad interrupted, "if Metatron starts listing his job duties, we'll still be here on Judgment Day." He grinned at his angel friend, who scowled in return.

Zad turned back to Allie. "We need to make a plan of attack, so to speak, so we can get this job done and get back to The City."

"I agree," Serariel said, his deep voice rumbling. "The army is not far from The City now. It would only take them days to reach the outer edge of the Gardens. I wish to be back within Abba's walls before they attack."

"Yeah okay," Allie agreed as she glanced at her friends — two humans, three angels and one bobcat who was casually cleaning demon blood from her fur. She laughed to herself; walking into Lucifer's camp and telling the soldiers that they've been deceived and should follow Abba instead was a suicide mission.

But hey, I'm always up for a challenge.

She then looked at the valley below them, an ocean of soldiers nearly as far as the eye could see. It reminded her of the Old Age, during the Tribulation and the final battle, when the antichrist's army had assembled together in a valley to fight against the last of Abba's believers.

Before that battle had even truly begun, Abba won. Every knee bowed and every tongue confessed that He was Lord. The same would happen with the millions of lost souls below.

She just hoped that they would make that confession before their time ran out, because this was truly their last chance.

Alejandro was once again barely restraining himself from barging into the tent city and start his yell-witnessing. Allie reminded him to stay close, to always be within reach of her or one of the angels. She made sure Duward understood the necessity for that too.

She'd had Duward keep the healing rod, since it seemed she was constantly getting injured and it was easier to have someone else do the healing. Plus, she thought it would give him a sense of purpose. He wasn't a warrior or a witness, so she figured he needed a job to feel useful.

"Okay, let's get started," Allie said once everyone was of the same mind. Since transferring could only be done to places you'd been before, Allie and the angels moved into the spirit and traveled throughout the entire camp. Even though it took much less time than it would have it they'd walked in physical bodies, it still took hours to get through the massive complex.

The plan was to transfer to the middle of the first grouping of tents, Alejandro would give his talk, then they'd transfer to the next grouping to the east and so on around the outer edge of the camp, then they would start moving inward, always moving in a circle. If anything happened, whoever was closest to Alejandro and Duward would grab them and they'd all transfer back to the top of the hill.

It wasn't normal to transfer into the midst of a group of people; it was too startling to humans to suddenly have people — and especially angels — appear out of nowhere. But under the circumstances, it was necessary. Time was running out and they needed to get the message delivered as quickly and to as many as possible.

Alejandro wasted no time. "Friends, we're sorry to startle you with our sudden appearance, but we have an important message for you. We have little time, so I will keep it simple: Lucifer has deceived you. He lied to you when he said you would conquer The City and live there. The truth is, he will be defeated once and for all when Abba throws him into the fiery lake. And all who chose to follow him and turn their backs on Abba will follow him there. Please reconsider your choice here — do not fall for the deception. Turn away now and seek Abba. He is ready to forgive you and accept you. You just have to ask."

There were murmurs among the men. Angry ones, from what Allie could tell. Her sword hand twitched with the desire to yank the weapon from the scabbard and give the idiots the option to choose Abba or die now. She had to remind herself that Abba wouldn't be pleased with that method.

"Come, we must move to the next group," Metatron murmured. Alejandro started to argue, but he stopped himself and with slumped shoulders, nodded. Allie felt sorry for him; nothing made the Chief Witness more despondent than to have the truth fall on deaf ears.

They transferred to the next group and Alejandro delivered almost the exact same message with nearly the same result.

He quickly became disheartened.

"I've been around since the beginning of man," Zad told him, putting his huge hand on Alejandro's shoulder. "Most don't accept the Good News right away, but many will accept it eventually."

Alejandro sighed and looked up at the angel. "I know, but the problem is these people don't *have* 'eventually'. Judgment is right around the corner."

The refusal to hear the truth continued in each group around the outer perimeter of the camp. Alejandro's message was getting more urgent each time, which Allie was glad for. She'd half-expected him to get despondent, but instead, he grew bolder.

And louder.

Things changed when they moved to the next ring. Suddenly, people were more receptive, at least willing to hear Abba's message and some even accepted His truth.

"Why do you think that is?" Allie asked Metatron as they stood at the outer edge of the group with Duward. Zad and Serariel were on either side of Alejandro, watching the crowd carefully. They'd had to transfer him away a few times in the outer ring of camps and even though the soldiers had been more receptive so far, they weren't taking any chances.

"Why what is?" the angel asked.

"That the soldiers are now at least letting Andro give his message, and some have even accepted it. Why them and not the others on the outer edge?"

The angel tilted his head in thought, but it was Duward who answered. "I think it's because those on the outer edge are newer to Lucifer's army. The closer we get to the inside, where people have been with him for the longest, I think we'll find they're aware of his lies and maybe they're tired of him."

Metatron nodded. "That makes sense. As people join the army, they would just set up camp on the outskirts."

The groups were larger in the next ring, but there were less camps. Allie noticed that a lot of soldiers on the outskirts of the camp were climbing on boxes and chairs in order to hear Alejandro. There were some who still looked angry at his message, but at least there seemed to be more who were willing to at least hear what he had to say.

Alejandro seemed to be recharged and instead of the yelling at people that he'd been doing, he was now telling them of Abba's love. Of His forgiveness. Allie found herself smiling and nodding.

"Excuse me... Mistress?" Allie turned at the voice to see a young man standing behind her. His wide eyes were darting between Metatron and Duward, both who had turned with her... *and they're both probably scowling at the poor guy,* she thought with a small smile.

"Yes?" Allie asked, hoping she sounded kind and not irritated at having her attention taken off of Alejandro. She reminded herself that he had two warrior angels watching over him, but after losing him in Kidal she wasn't too keen on letting him out of her sight.

The man took a hesitant step closer, his nervous eyes darting over the guys again. Allie sighed.

"It's okay, boys, I got this," she told them as she moved closer to the guy. Even if the man attacked her, she knew she could easily take him. Humans were easy to fight; it was the demons — and especially the fallen angels — that were difficult.

Just in case, though, she glanced down at the man's hands to make sure he wasn't holding onto some Pit shackles.

"What can I do for you?" she asked him softly as she shifted her shield to her side. *See? Not a threat. I'm not even trying to defend myself here...*

He swallowed and took another hesitant step closer. He was a thin man, light-skinned and green-eyed with sandy hair. His skin was so pale it was almost white, except for red patches of color high on his cheeks.

"Uh, well, I um, I was there... in Kidal. The day that, uh, Lucifer and you, um... you know."

Allie laughed. "The day I kicked Lucifer's butt on the stage in front of a million people?" she asked as she crossed her arms over her chest. That would always be one of her finer moments.

The man nodded with a slight smile. "Yes, but after, when you came off the stage and told everyone who could hear about Abba. About the truth." He nodded toward Alejandro.

"Like he's doing now." His nervous eyes darted around the area, as if seeing who was listening. He leaned closer. "I heard you. I believed."

Allie's eyes widened. "Then why are you still here?"

He glanced around again. "I wanted to go to the Paradise Gardens. Some of my family did. But my father and my brother, they insisted we stay with the army. They're afraid of Lucifer."

Allie refrained from rolling her eyes. "They really should be more afraid of Abba, and of the judgment that's coming. Then it will be too late to decide where your loyalties are."

The man nodded. "I know. I was hoping, um, if you could tell my father this? I've tried, but he will not listen to me."

Allie hesitated; it could be another trap, another opportunity to catch the Mistress, to lock some more of the stupid shackles on her. Instincts told her that the guy was telling the truth, but she wasn't going to be careless. Not again, anyway. She turned and walked back to the guys.

"Hey," she said to Metatron as she tapped him on the shoulder. He turned his head and glanced down at her. "I need to go with this guy. You guys wanna go with me?"

The angel looked over her head at the guy she'd been talking to. Allie didn't look back, but she imagined the poor man's pale complexion just whitened further at having the huge angel's attention focused on him.

Metatron looked back at her and nodded. "Wait here," he told her, then he glanced at Duward, unspoken communication passing between them. Allie bristled at them thinking she was the "little woman who needs protecting," but she really couldn't complain. First, they cared about her well-being; and second, recent history showed she had a knack for getting captured and kind of needed protecting.

So, she'd suck it up and let them watch over her. It was definitely better than being in Lucifer's grasp again.

Allie walked back to the guy who looked like he was going to be sick. "Is he c-c-coming with us?" he stammered. She laughed.

"Don't let his scowls intimidate you. Metatron is a pussycat, for the most part." She leaned close to him. "Just don't tell him I called him that," she said with a wink.

The guy huffed out a nervous laugh and Allie stuck out her hand as Duward turned and approached them.

"I'm Allie and this is Duward," she told him.

"Nels," the guy responded as he shook their hands. "Thank you for agreeing to this. My father is, um, well, he's difficult. Stubborn. He wouldn't listen when I told him the truth."

Allie nodded as she watched Metatron trotting back toward them. "Well, I'm not a witness, but we'll see what I can do."

"If nothing else, she can nag them into leaving the army," Metatron drawled.

Chapter 16

NELS' FATHER WAS a rather imposing man. Allie was once again surprised to encounter a large human. While Lars wasn't nearly as tall as Duward, the older man was a good six inches taller than Allie. But what made him truly imposing was his scowl; it could have rivaled Metatron's at his grumpiest.

Allie was surprised to learn that Lars was a leader in the army, a sort of captain, with ten thousand men under him.

The man was antagonistic at first when Allie started to tell him the truth. But she could tell it wasn't because he didn't believe what she was saying, but that he really was afraid of Lucifer, of what he could do, like Nels had said.

"But consider this," Allie argued, "angering Lucifer has temporary consequences. But angering Abba — by choosing to follow His enemy — has eternal consequences. You've screwed yourself up for, like, ever."

Duward snorted behind her and Allie jabbed her elbow back at him without looking. Lars rubbed his chin as he contemplated Allie's words. Finn, Nels' brother, bristled.

"Papa, you can't be considering leaving the army," he huffed. "You know what will happen if we leave—"

"Hush," Lars said and he looked at Nels. "Are you willing to risk it?"

Nels glanced at Allie before answering. She wondered what "it" was that he was going to risk. Nels nodded.

"Yes. I told you before that I don't care what Lucifer does to us, or to—" he swallowed and looked down. "Each person has to make their own choices."

Lars sighed and ran a weary hand over his face. He started to speak, but Allie interrupted.

"Hold up. I'm well aware of what that douche canoe is capable of. Exactly what is it he threatened you with?"

Lars glanced at Nels and Finn. It was Finn who spoke up. "The 'douche canoe,' as you call him," his lips twitched at that, "threatened our families. Our mother, sisters and our children. Said he would rape the females and enslave them all."

Allie looked at Metatron. "Can I just go kill him now?" The angel crossed his arms over his chest and gave her look.

She sighed and turned back to the men. "Guess not. Anyway, is he holding your families?" The men shook their heads.

"Well, seems like his threats are pretty stupid then," Allie shrugged and waved her hand to indicate the army camp. "He probably told most of the soldiers here the same thing. The threat seems scary, I know, but think about it... can Lucifer *really* kill all the families? Seriously... he's got his evil plans to fulfill, trying to gather an army to attack Abba." She snorted.

"Like that's going to work out. C'mon, Abba is the freaking *Creator of the universe,* for Pete's sake! There's no way Lucifer, who is a created being — created *by Abba* — is going to win against Him."

Lars looked like he was contemplating her words again. She waited for a moment to let him digest what she'd said.

"Look, you leave here and go get your families and head to The City. Abba will accept you with open arms. Honestly, He can't wait for His children to come to Him. When you've made that decision to accept Him, accept His offer, there isn't anything Lucifer can do to you to change that."

Allie sensed Duward listening carefully to her words. She hoped he was getting the message too.

"Lucifer can kill your body," Metatron added, "torture you, rape your women—"

"Not helping, dude," Allie muttered. The angel looked at her, then actually seemed embarrassed.

"No matter what he does to your physical body," he amended, "your soul is Abba's once you accept Him. There is *nothing* Lucifer can do to change that."

Lars, Nels and Finn seemed to digest that for several moments. Finally, Lars spoke.

"You're right. The first thing we must do is go to our families and tell them this good news. Tell them that Abba wants us."

Allie grinned. "Oh, He doesn't just *want* you," she told them, "He longs for you. You're His children. He's been waiting for you to come home for your entire life."

~~

After Allie's talk with Lars, he and his sons gladly made the decision to leave the army. With Lars' influence as a captain, several thousand of those under his command chose to leave also.

Alejandro had great success in his witnessing too, so much so that the angels were angsty, worried that Lucifer was going to start noticing that his followers were no longer following.

They made their way through the second circle much more quickly than they had the outer circle — partly because it was smaller than the outer circle, but also because it was much easier to convince people to leave — and then they moved on to the third circle.

After that, there were only two more circles and then they'd be at the center of the camp. And where Lucifer was.

The angels and Duward grew more tense with each stop. Alejandro was seeing great success in reaching the people with Abba's message, but as Lucifer's army shrunk, it was obvious something —

or someone — was causing the desertions.

"We need to stay together," Metatron warned just as they transferred to a new group. "The demons will be investigating the desertions." He looked pointedly at Allie. "I do not wish to rescue you again."

Allie stuck her tongue out at him. It might not have been the most mature thing the Mistress of the Remnant Warriors could have done, but it made her feel better. The angel smirked in response and blew her a kiss.

Metatron... blew me a kiss. Allie shook her head. The universe must have shifted somewhere. In response, she punched his arm.

Serariel had volunteered to lead the "deserters" to The City and Duward offered to go with him. Even though it meant less big dudes to help keep an eye on things, Allie was thankful. It was going to be a time-consuming task for them, with having to stop at communities along the way in order to collect the soldiers' families. But it was a worthwhile job, for sure.

Because people in the Inner Circle and Outer Zone didn't have the benefit of the Living Waters and Tree of Life to heal them, they often suffered from disease and injuries. For that reason, Allie insisted that Duward take the healing rod with him.

"But what if you or the others are injured again?" Duward had argued.

Allie shrugged. "We're not fighting, remember? If

anything happens, we're transferring out of there."

And once they'd left the outer ring of the army camp, things had gone so smoothly that it made Allie nervous. In her experience nothing *ever* went the way it was supposed to and when it did... well, she was waiting for all hell to break loose.

Literally.

They were in the third circle and on the fifth group. Alejandro had just finished his speech and hundreds of soldiers had made the decision to follow Abba. Allie had estimated that nearly a million soldiers had deserted so far. Not a small number, but considering the army probably numbered twenty million, the percentages weren't great.

There were just too many willing to follow the liar and not *The Truth.*

"Well, that went okay, I guess," Alejandro said when he'd joined Allie and the others after his latest "hot talk" as Allie called it. Alejandro had a tendency to talk about the "fire and brimstone" aftermath of Judgment Day, rather than the love and forgiveness of Abba, like she constantly encouraged him to share.

In her opinion, Abba's unconditional love and grace were much more amazing than His capability of destroying.

"Yeah, you reeled in a lot of fish," Allie told her friend. Thousands more had chosen to leave the army during Alejandro's last speech. Not only those who'd heard, but those who'd been told the story by their fellow soldiers and had seen the mass exodus from Lucifer's army.

It was truly amazing and inspiring how many had chosen to side with Abba. To deal with all of them, Serariel and Duward were going to take those who'd already made the decision to the far edge of the Inner Circle. Then Duward would stay with them while Serariel transferred back to the army to collect the new believers and their families along the way once again.

Zad brought a tray piled with food for them. Metatron instantly reached for a pastry, but Allie playfully slapped his hand away and handed him a fig instead.

"You're getting fat, dude," she said around a mouthful of mango. "Could barely hold you up back in the demon dungeon."

A mixture of shock and alarm crossed the big angel's face. He ran a hand down his muscular torso, realizing quickly that Allie was just messing with him. She grinned when he scowled at her.

"I'm not fat," he muttered. She laughed when he picked up the fig instead.

They were nearly done eating when shouts of panic had them instantly on their feet, swords drawn.

"Demons!" a soldier shouted. Allie groaned. She just hated being right about the easy success being the calm before the satanic storm.

"Where's Alejandro?" Zad asked.

Allie mentally kicked herself; she hadn't been paying close enough attention to the Chief Witness, who had a tendency to wander. She'd been more interested in eating and giving Metatron a hard time.

Instead of answering, she shouted his name. They couldn't transfer without him and with all the demons coming their way, the odds of fighting them off wasn't in their favor.

Alejandro poked his head out of a tent just as three demons passed. Allie widened her eyes at him and gave a quick jerk of her head, telling him to go back inside, out of sight. Thankfully, the demons hadn't paid any attention to him, with their focus on the angels and her.

Being outnumbered wasn't usually an issue for the angels, who could turn into giants at any time. But the trouble was, the demons could do the same and there would be a lot of collateral human damage if they decided to duke it out Goliath style.

One good thing was that demons didn't carry weapons, so it was easy to cut them down with a sword before they got close enough to disembowel with their claws. But they were sneaky, fought dirty and ganged up on their opponent.

Like the jerks are doing now, Allie thought when four demons rushed at her. With one smooth strike, she cut the head off the nearest one, wincing when his blood splattered her. Nothing she hated more than blood, but demon blood... it made her want to strip her uniform off and jump into the nearest vat of lye.

She jerked when she felt claws raking across her torso and mentally cheered Abba's design of her uniform, which was thankfully demon claw-proof. It didn't protect her head, though, which the demon obviously figured out when he swiped at her face. She cried out when she felt the burn of his claws down her cheek.

Allie sensed Metatron turning toward her and cursed herself for crying out, drawing his attention away from his own fight. From the corner of her eye, she could see the pair were fighting about a dozen demons on their own; they certainly didn't need her distracting them.

"I'm fine!" she yelled without taking her eyes off her opponents. "Eyes on your own fight!"

The problem was, she *wasn't* fine. Once the demons realized her uniform was protecting her, the three remaining started clawing at her head. It was all she could do to keep them from shredding her face completely off.

Even though Allie knew many of the soldiers watching the fight were new believers, none joined in the fight to help them. She had to fight back anger and resentment at that, reminding herself that they were rightfully fearful of the demons and didn't yet grasp the fact that no matter what happened to them now, they would be with Abba forever.

With her back against the angels, she couldn't get into an offensive position to fight. It was all she could do to defend herself, so she turned to the side and backed away from her friends a few paces. If one of the demons turned to attack the angels from behind, she'd still be close enough to take him out before he did.

From her new position, she was able to do more damage with wider sword swings. She caught one demon in the arm, lopping it off at the shoulder and another took a stab through the ribs.

That left only one, and Allie liked those odds a lot better. She whipped the sword in front of her in short arcs, so fast the metal was a shiny blur. The demon backed up and Allie followed, intent on taking his head.

The demon knew he wasn't going to win; she could see the realization in his eyes. Why he didn't turn and run was a good question, but when a grin crossed his face as he looked over her shoulder, she had her answer.

More demons had come up behind her.

She did a half turn to put her side to the new attackers, but it was too late. One swept her legs out from under her and she landed on her back, knocking the breath out of her.

They were on her immediately, clawing at her. Pain seared through Allie's face, neck and scalp as she did all she could to cover her face and fight them off, but it was impossible.

She was going to bleed to death.

A deafening roar drew the demons' attention away for a split second, long enough for Allie to thrust the one straddling her chest with her sword. A strangled gurgle escaped him before he coughed blood in her face, then fell to the side.

"Great," Allie griped, "demon blood now mixed with mine. Evil cooties, just what I need."

She saw the source of the roar when Metatron's sword stabbed a demon to her side and she started to push herself up to help him, but a couple more demons came up then to join the fight and the angel moved to stand over her.

Allie's heart warmed at his protection, despite the fact that it stung that she needed it. She realized then that it was a very, *very* good thing that Abba was going to fight — and win — the final battle, because no amount of training by the Remnants could have prepared them to fight an onslaught of demons.

Since she couldn't stand and fight, Allie did what she could to stab feet and slice Achilles tendons. Hobbling demons turned out to be pretty effective, because they were dropping left and right, howling like wounded animals.

Her efforts weren't enough though. There were just too many of the enemy and they seemed to keep coming. Metatron must have realized it too, because he glanced down at her while still fighting.

"Transfer out of here!" he ordered.

"Not without you!" Allie yelled back as she jabbed her sword into the kneecap of a demon who'd been about to stab Metatron in the thigh.

"Stubborn woman!" Metatron roared back. "It is too dangerous for you here!"

"Oh, like it's not for you!" she shot back. She almost reminded him about the fact that Abba had changed the demons' anatomy during the Releasing in order to allow them to be killed. But to do so, he'd also changed the angels' in order to keep balance. But she kept her mouth shut because she wasn't sure if the demons were aware that the angels could die now.

Definitely didn't need to alert them to that.

Metatron growled like a bear but didn't continue arguing. He was too busy trying to keep her safe. Now that she wasn't being torn apart by demon claws, she wanted to get back in the fight and give them a little payback. Or a lot, actually.

Allie pushed back, crawling out from between the angel's legs and rolled to her feet. Zad was busy fighting his own horde and she tried to decide who needed her help the most. They both did, equally from what she could see.

"Hey!" she yelled to draw the demons' attention and wasn't surprised when every demon looked her way, two losing their heads thanks to the distraction of having the Mistress so close. She knew the demons were after her. Lucifer wanted her more than anything else, except for maybe Abba's City.

A handful of demons abandoned their fight with the angels and headed toward her. She was still outnumbered and now that she was injured with blood dripping in her eyes it was going to make fighting even more difficult. But she had to do what she could to keep her angel friends from getting hurt.

Or worse.

The demons surged toward her and she managed to take several out before they surrounded her again. Allie knew she wasn't going to make it through this battle. In the best case, she'd be killed. The worst, captured.

She'd run her own sword through her belly before that happened again.

While she knew there wasn't a chance that she'd win, Allie fought with everything she had. She hoped she could at least even out the odds so the angels would stand a chance at getting away with Alejandro. And even though they could have used the help, she was glad Serariel and Duward were safely away.

"That's right, whine like a little girl," she taunted as a demon howled after she sliced him up. Another demon's head fell at her feet and another fell back, his chest cut open.

But still they came. Allie was growing tired, and

she was regretting not being able to practice with her fellow Remnants as much as she would have liked. Her stamina certainly wasn't what it used to be.

The demons managed to get around behind her once again and were clawing at the back of her head. Allie knew it was just moments now, before they overwhelmed her. She welcomed death. She was just too tired, had lost too much blood, to keep fighting.

A demon drew back his hand and Allie lowered her sword in defeat, too weak to defend herself any longer. But before he could make contact, Metatron barged into the circle, putting himself between her and the demon. The claws meant for her throat ripped across the angel's chest and he howled in pain as he removed the demon's head.

Her friend fought valiantly, and Allie wanted so much to help him, but the blood running from her wounds filled her eyes as the weakness overcame her. She sank to her knees as she made pathetic, ineffective swipes with her sword, causing the demons to laugh.

The beautiful sword Abba had created just for her felt like a huge stone in her hand. Allie tried to hang on to it, but the effort was too great. She whimpered as it slipped from her grasp and a demon snatched it up.

Complete and utter defeat.

Despite her acceptance of impending death, she couldn't help but flinch at the sounds of flesh being sliced and the grunts of pain that surrounded her.

As she slumped in the dirt, Allie wondered how many more demons there were. If Zad had triumphed. And how Metatron was doing in his own fight, the fight he'd taken on when she'd failed.

Zad cried out then and Allie forced her head up. The angel was staring in her direction with a look of horror. He then jumped over a demon body, heading toward her. She frowned slightly, wondering if she looked that bad, but then someone slammed into her, knocking her over.

Allie rolled to her side and blinked several times, trying to clear the blood out of her eyes. She blinked a few more times, sure that her eyes were playing tricks on her. But no... Metatron was lying next to her, staring back.

Except his head was no longer attached to his body.

Chapter 17

N O! METATRON, NO!" Allie screamed, but it came out barely a whisper. *No, no, no... not you. It's supposed to be me. Oh, Abba, please, no!* As soon as the words left her mind, she felt Abba's presence, trying to offer comfort.

But it wasn't comfort she wanted; she needed her friend back.

Blood and tears filling her eyes, Allie used the last of her strength to extend a trembling hand to touch the face of the angel who'd been so hard on her, pushing her beyond her limits, angering her with his bossiness.

But he had loved her with just as much passion as he'd put into training her. And now he was dead, his head removed by her own sword, in a fight that hadn't been his. All because he'd been trying to protect her.

His final act of love.

A vague awareness of an avenging angel finishing off the last of the demons tickled her mind as she started to fall off into the blackness. *Thank Abba Zad wasn't taken too...* She felt her body floating then, voices around her, a touch on her face. She knew Zad was trying to save her.

Let me go. I want to go... be with Metatron...

~~

"Allie... Allie... Alessandra!"

The light hurt her eyes and she had to blink a few times to get them to adjust. Surrounded by fluffy comfort, she wondered where she was. Certainly not in the army camp, where the softest thing to be found was turned dirt. Not in their own camp, which was also lacking much comfort. *Even the contrans' seats aren't as soft as this.*

"Daughter."

Abba's voice caused Allie to turn her head. But He wasn't there. In His place was Zad, with a worried look on his beautiful face. He smiled, but it didn't reach his eyes.

"Where—" The word came out as a croak, so she tried to clear her throat. "Where are we?"

"In the mansion," a new voice said. She turned her head and smiled.

"Nick," she breathed as she reached out a hand to her husband. He took it and kissed the back of her fingers.

"Welcome back, love," he said, his own voice catching. "We almost lost..." his voice trailed off and he looked away, but not before Allie noticed the shine in his eyes.

It was then that she remembered Metatron. And

the horrible way he died. She sucked in a pained breath.

"Metatron," she whispered as she threw her forearm over her face. Absently she noted that she didn't hurt anymore; someone must have healed her. Physically, anyway.

"Yeah," Zad said, sadness coloring his voice. "Sucks." A hand covered hers on the bed.

"He's not gone, you know. Just resting. Won't be long before we see him again."

Allie nodded; she knew that, but like the others who'd died prematurely, it was still hard to let go of the sorrow at the loss. Especially when she had guilt piled on top of it.

A vibration against her side caused her to drop the arm covering her face. "Hey girl," Allie whispered to Charu as she reached down to scratch her behind the ears.

"She insisted on coming from The City when she heard," Nick said softly, his hand joining Allie's to stroke the cat's soft fur.

Allie huffed out a breath. "I'm surprised anyone would want to be around me, considering I'm the reason Meta—" her voice caught on a sob and she covered her face with both hands.

"Hey, don't," Zad said as he pulled her up into his arms. Allie sobbed into her angel friend's chest as Nick shifted so he could wrap his arms around her from behind. Despite her agony, she felt wrapped up in so much love it was almost overwhelming.

"It wasn't your fault, so don't even go there. What he did was instinctual. Metatron adored you, you know," Zad murmured, his arms tightening around her. "He couldn't stand the thought of you hurting, even when it was just a scratch you'd gotten in practice. He watched over you like a hawk and had begged Abba to be your guardian."

He laughed then. "The other angels teased him about it constantly. Called you 'Minitron'. And, okay, I may or may not have started that nickname."

A chuckle escaped her at that; she had no idea Metatron had felt that way about her. She knew the stoic angel had cared about her and loved her, but not that he was *that* protective.

They were quiet for a long while, lost in their own thoughts. It was Nick who broke the silence.

"I think that Metatron gave himself for you gladly. It was an honorable death in his eyes. Sacrificing himself to save you. The ultimate love. Just as Abba did for us on the cross."

Allie's eyes filled again as she nodded against Zad's chest. They were both right, and while it didn't stop the pain, it did help with the guilt.

"It is but a short while before you will be with him again, daughter. Take heart."

Allie smiled. *Thanks Daddy. I love You and miss You.*

"I love you too, child. Always. Continue your fight. The battle is almost done."

~~

Since they were now down two angels and one large human, Abba allowed Nick and Charo to accompany Allie and Zad back to the army. He'd then called the rest of the Remnants to the Gardens to set up a defense for the upcoming attack.

After Zad had taken Allie to the Remnant mansion for healing, he'd transferred Alejandro to Serariel and Duward so that the Chief Witness could share the truth with the new believers' families.

Serariel had hugged Allie for a very long time and whispered in her ear, repeating what Zad had said, encouraging her to push aside any guilt feelings and to concentrate on the task ahead.

"Not for one second that I hung from Lucifer's shackles in the blackness did I regret giving myself so that you could live," he'd told her. "And I know my brother felt exactly the same."

With some difficulty, Allie shoved down the guilt and turned it into anger at the demons and of course Lucifer. They were the cause of all the bad... and they needed to pay for that.

She knew that they'd be paying for all eternity, of course. But she planned on making them suffer in the here and now too.

It was with renewed purpose that Allie pushed

the small team to move through the camp as quickly as possible. After completing the third ring, Nick suggested they change their strategy and start appearing to different groups in what would appear to be a more random fashion. He argued that would throw the demons off, making it harder to predict where they were going to show up.

Allie argued that she *wanted* the demons to find them, because she had a vendetta. The others just gave her a look that spoke volumes.

She estimated that they'd reached three-quarters of the army so far, and possibly a quarter of them had chosen to desert and move to the safety of The City. Not a great number when you looked at percentages but considering the fact that the army had grown to nearly twenty-three million soldiers, Allie thought five or so million new believers wasn't too shabby.

Of course, that also meant millions more people were going to end up on the wrong side come Judgment Day, a fact that made her heart ache.

Some of the seemingly random transfers — that were actually carefully mapped out by Nick — brought them far too close to Lucifer's camp for comfort. Having spent months with the jerk and being terrified of getting stuck with him again, Allie was extremely antsy.

"Hurry up," she hissed to Alejandro when he'd spent longer than she thought he should with his speech.

Nick gave her a confused look. "He's only been talking for about three minutes."

Charo walked over and sat on Allie's feet, which she'd come to realize was the cat's way of offering comfort. She reached down and pet her, never taking her eyes off the crowd. She just knew another horde of demons was going to pop out and attack their far too small party.

Zad stepped closer to her and wrapped his arm around her shoulders. "He's not going to get you again. I'll kill you before I let him," he quipped with a grin.

Allie arched her eyebrow at him. "Gee, thanks. I feel so much better," she drawled as she elbowed him.

But his joke wasn't funny, because if Zad didn't kill her if Lucifer grabbed her, she'd impale herself on her own sword.

The second the words "If you choose to believe the truth, Abba greatly desires you to come to Him. You just need to leave this place and make your way to The City," left Alejandro's mouth, Allie grabbed him and Charo and transferred them to their newest safe base, the location of which Nick insisted they change daily. In just a moment, Nick and Zad joined them.

"Nervous much?" Zad joked, but Nick was frowning.

He turned to the angel. "I don't like this either.

You know Lucifer wants Allie. He's threatened to wear her head when he attacks!" he said with an angry gesture.

"It's getting too hard to defend Andro and watch for demons, or worse, Lucifer himself. There just aren't enough of us for the job, especially now that the demons are actively seeking us."

Allie nodded in agreement. Just the day before, they'd cut Alejandro short when they spotted demons running their way. She was just thankful that so far none of the demons with the invisibility power had shown up. The only way to see them was through the spirit, but she couldn't watch everything else when she was in the distracting spirit world.

Zad stood with his arms crossed over his chest as he thought over Nick's argument. "Let's call it a day—"

"Wait, what?" Alejandro interrupted. "We've barely started! I only witnessed to three groups so far and we still have a few dozen to reach!"

Zad put his hand out in a "hushing" gesture. "I know. But I have a plan that will fix all our problems and, honestly, I feel kinda dumb for not thinking of it sooner. I just have to run it by Abba first for His approval."

"Oh, hey, if you're going to The City, bring back some of those swiss chard pies that Trenton makes, would you?" Allie asked.

"Ooh, yeah, and some oranges," Alejandro added.

"I haven't had any citrus in a long time."

"I could use some chocolate," Nick chimed in.

Zad rolled his eyes at the humans. "I'm not Uber Eats, for crying out loud," they heard as he transferred.

~~

When Zad returned that evening — with groceries in hand — he shared his idea and said that Abba had given His okay.

Allie poked her angel friend in the ribs as they sat eating the goodies. "You're right. You should have thought of this sooner. We coulda been back in The City by now, eating like this every day," she said as she popped a grape in her mouth.

Zad smirked. "Well, considering I wasn't even supposed to be here with you, it probably wouldn't have been a good idea to finish the job in such a short time. Kinda hard to explain."

"So what are we gonna do while you and Andro are off on your adventure? Just hang out and sunbathe?" Nick joked. Allie laughed, glad that her husband who had always been so sober had gotten much easier going. *Just like Metatron...*

She absently rubbed her chest, wincing at the ache that settled in her heart whenever she thought of her friend. Nick must have sensed it, because he took her other hand and tugged her closer, kissing her neck.

"It's okay, baby. We'll all be together again real soon." Allie sighed and nodded.

"You're going to be the ground crew," Zad said around a mouthful of pastry. Another reminder of Metatron. But this time, it made her smile, remembering that she'd teased him about getting fat and how indignant he'd gotten.

She couldn't wait to give the big guy a hard time again.

"Ground crew?" Allie asked. "Like eyes on the sky?"

Zad grinned. "Yep. Still gotta watch for demons, but at least you won't be worrying about Alejandro at the time."

The angel's plan was to fly Alejandro above the camp where he could witness to those below. He'd teased Alejandro that with his loud mouth, he should be able to reach the last half mile of camps they had left all in one shot.

Zad pointed to the map Nick had made of the camp. "Right here is where we'll transfer and make sure we have everyone's attention before I fly us up above the crowd."

He waved a breadstick between Allie and Nick. "You two—"

"Meeerowrrr," Charo protested loudly, looking up from the cabbage she'd been chewing on.

Zad smiled at the cat. "Sorry, gorgeous. You

three transfer to the edge of this group of camps right here," he said as he used his breadstick to point to another area on the map. "No one will be paying attention to you, guaranteed."

He hooked thumb at Alejandro. "Especially not when the human broadcast system here starts yelling at them."

Alejandro tucked his chin and gave the angel a look of disbelief. "Seriously?"

"He's not wrong," Nick drawled, and they all laughed. Even Charo chuckled.

~~

Early the next morning when the enemy army was just starting their daily training, the group got into position. Zad warned Allie and Nick to make sure they warned him if they saw any demons. Even though demons preferred their claws to weapons, the soldiers were certainly armed and could shoot at the angel and Chief.

It still irritated Allie that Lucifer had managed to stockpile firearms from the Old Age. Abba hadn't been surprised when she'd told Him, though. And it didn't matter anyway; Abba was going to kick Lucifer's evil butt regardless of what weapon he might bring to the battle.

But the last thing they needed was some soldier shooting at Zad and Alejandro before he'd finished witnessing to the entire army. They had figured that the soldiers would be too enthralled to see an angel flying, and too focused on what Alejandro was saying, to shoot at them. But that didn't mean a demon couldn't swipe a gun and do so himself.

Zad and Alejandro transferred, Nick and Allie waited until they saw him soar into the sky before transferring themselves. They made it a point to appear behind a large tent on the outskirts of the tent groupings. Unfortunately, the ground in the area was fairly flat, so they couldn't see very far.

"Would be nice to have the angel's stretchy thing, huh?" Allie murmured.

"'Stretchy thing'?" Nick snorted, then nodded. "Yeah, it would be good to be able to see over these tents."

They stared out over the crowd looking up, most with their mouths open in awe. Allie glanced up; Zad was hovering above the crowd, his huge wings flapping gently to keep them in place. To top it off and make himself even more visible, he was glowing.

Seeing an angel flying was pretty amazing, Allie had to admit, especially with the glow making swirls around his body like the Aurora Borealis. It reminded her of the spiritual realm...

She tilted her head to the side in thought. "Hey," she murmured to her husband, "do me a favor and watch over me. I'm gonna go into the spirit and go around the camp to see if I spot any demons."

Nick looked like he didn't like the idea, but he nodded, and Allie entered the otherworldly realm.

Forcing herself to focus on her task, she moved in between the tents, passing through a few. They were covering a much larger area with Alejandro's witnessing — which *did* sound like it was being broadcast through speakers, she thought with a chuckle — so there was a lot more area to cover.

From her peripherals, she noticed Charo trotting a few tents away in a parallel pattern. The cat looked at her and winked and Allie laughed. Apparently, animals could see spirits. She'd always wondered about that.

She'd made it almost all the way around the circle when she spotted a horde of demons running toward the crowd. Without thought, Allie moved to Zad. *Cool trick,* she thought. She had no idea she could "fly" in the spirit too.

Zad was focused on the crowd below, his gorgeous blue eyes scanning the crowd. But he didn't see the horde that was coming up from behind. Allie wasn't sure if she could get his attention since he was so focused, but she thought it was worth a try.

"Zad," she tried to whisper in his ear, but there really wasn't any sound. *"Zad!"* she thought-yelled, but he didn't even flinch. Allie sighed in frustration and wondered if her body on the ground actually made the sound.

In a last-ditch effort, she pushed her spirit into Zad, hoping he'd at least feel her. She wondered if it would be cold, like the Old Age humans always claimed when a ghost was near.

Instead of surrounding him, though, she actually entered him. Suddenly seeing out of Zad's eyes was shocking, to say the least. She thought her New Age enhanced eyes were awesome, but an angel's eyes were far cooler.

Even though they were several stories above them, every detail of the humans below was vivid, from the tiny beads of sweat on upper lips to the loose threads on uniforms and specks of dirt on shoes.

"Wow," Allie said, but it came out of Zad's mouth. She felt him startle.

"What the—"

Oops... Allie forced herself to leave his body and was instantly confronted with a shocked and somewhat angry angel.

"What the heck, Allie?" Zad scowled at her.

She shrugged. *"Sorry. Didn't mean to do that. I wanted to warn you that a horde is coming up."* She pointed in the direction she'd seen them. *"Better wrap it up."*

Zad nodded, and then she returned to her body, and her husband.

But Nick wasn't there.

Chapter 18

ALEJANDRO'S MESSAGE via angel carrier was much more effective than any other message he'd given in his lifetime. Soldiers left Lucifer's camp in droves. It should have thrilled Allie, but she was too worried about Nick and what had happened to him.

When she'd returned to her body, she found that she'd been shoved under the back of a tent. Nick had probably been trying to hide her while she was moving around in the spirit. She immediately transferred to their designated safe base, but no one was there. Before she could transfer directly to Nick, though, Zad appeared with Alejandro.

"Nick's gone!" she told them. "I'm going to transfer to him."

Zad's hand shot out and grabbed her arm. "Hold on. Don't do that. If he's been captured, you'll be stepping right into a trap."

Allie growled in frustration. She hated that he was right. She wanted nothing more than to find Nick and rescue him. Especially if he was in Lucifer's custody. But getting herself caught again wouldn't do anyone any good.

And Nick would be really angry.

"Alright, but let me at least go to him in the

spirit."

It took a little bit because she wasn't as good at finding her loved ones in the spirit as she was at transferring to them. But once she did find him — chained up with the stupid Pit shackles and a little bloody, but otherwise unharmed — Allie relaxed a little.

And Zad had been right — Nick was heavily guarded. It would have been suicide to transfer to him, especially since she wouldn't have been able to transfer him out with the chains on him.

Lucifer was going to want revenge on the deserters — and especially on those who'd encouraged them to leave. It made Allie sick to know that Nick was at his mercy… and everyone knew Lucifer didn't have a merciful bone in his body. It made her sick to leave him, but there wasn't anything she could do at the moment.

"Let's just finish up here, stop off at Serariel and Duward to let them know they're about to be overrun with new believers and then we'll go see what Abba has to say."

Allie reluctantly nodded and then at Zad's insistence, she and Charo waited at the safe base while Zad flew Alejandro over the rest of the camp. They weren't even gone twenty minutes when they returned. Alejandro's wide grin told her everything she needed to know.

"You were successful, I take it?"

Alejandro laughed. "And then some. I think almost half of the soldiers closest to Lucifer's base camp deserted."

Zad was grinning too. "And Lucifer wasn't happy. We flew over him just as he grabbed a gun to start shooting. I, uh, may or may not have given him a certain Old Age hand gesture."

"Zad!" Allie scolded as she whacked him with the back of her hand. "We're not supposed to stoop to his level."

He laughed. "I know, but you should have seen the look on his face. Priceless."

They hurriedly transferred to the others and apprised them of the situation. Alejandro and Charo both wanted to stay with Serariel and Duward, so Allie and Zad wished them well and encouraged them to hurry to The City.

Abba seemed to be waiting for them. As soon as they transferred to the Throne Room, He stepped forward and engulfed Allie in His arms.

"You've done well, daughter," He murmured. Allie laughed, but it wasn't a humorous sound.

"Don't know about that," she said into His warm chest. "I lost Alejandro — twice — then because of me, the angels were beat up. And now Nick's been captured. On top of that, I almost died but Metatron—" her voice broke and she started sobbing. Abba's arms tightened around her.

"It's alright, child. He's resting now. You'll see

him soon. Very soon, actually."

Allie nodded, then Abba kissed her cheek and set her away, holding her at arm's length. He gave her a tiny shake.

"Now, you have a new mission. Gather your team and set up camp in the Gardens. Recruit as many of Lucifer's soldiers that you can. You only have less than a month to get a line of defense organized."

Allie's eyes widened. "A month? That's it?" she squeaked. She had no idea that the attack was so close. Abba nodded.

"Lucifer has gathered all he's going to." He grinned then. "And thanks to you and Alejandro, he has a lot less than he thought he'd get."

"Hey, a little appreciation for the Heavenly Host who helped," Zad drawled and Abba turned to him with an arched eyebrow.

"You mean the Heavenly Host who weren't supposed to intervene? *That* Heavenly Host?"

Allie laughed when Zad's cheeks colored, but he grinned at the Father. "Well, since You put it that way..."

Abba shook His head, but was smiling. "I'm always surrounding Myself with insubordinates." He pointed at Zad. "You will be punished, but I haven't yet decided how."

Allie started to protest, but Abba held up His hand. "Justice, my child. The angels knew they would be punished."

He leaned toward her then and whispered in her ear. "I think I'll make him peel potatoes in the kitchens for a month." Allie grinned at that image. Even though she didn't want Zad punished at all, that was pretty mild.

A slight frown crossed her face then as she thought about the huge task Abba had just given her. She'd need all the angelic help she could get to pull it off.

"Can I have the angels' help for building the line?" *Please, please, please.* The project was just too big for her to even think about.

Abba laughed. "Yes, I have already told the Host to be prepared for this."

That was a relief, but it was still such a huge undertaking that she had no clue where to start. Even though she was technically in charge of all the Remnants, this was way above her head. Nick was the strategist.

"So, what can we do about Nick?"

Abba turned away and moved to sit on the steps leading to His throne. Allie sat next to Him, but Zad remained standing. It was something she'd never quite gotten used to — the angels had been with Abba long before man's creation, yet Abba was more intimate with the humans.

It was definitely more a Father-child type of relationship.

Abba didn't say anything and seemed to be thinking, which was kind of weird considering He had all knowledge of all things. Allie wasn't getting a good feeling. It seemed like He was delaying telling her what she wanted — needed — to hear.

His shoulders lifted and Allie wondered if it was due to a sigh she couldn't hear. "It isn't going to be safe to get him," He said, and Allie's heart sunk. She was going to have to just turn her back on her husband.

Abba chuckled. "Hold on, don't get your back fur up," He said with a grin, as always reading her mind. "I didn't say it couldn't be done, but it certainly is dangerous. I do not want you going in, but I will send Duward since he isn't known like you are and he can dress as a soldier to blend in." He motioned to the angel standing before them.

"I'll also send Zad with him, disguised as another soldier."

The argument that had been on Allie's lips about sending Duward alone died off. Having Zad at his side would obviously be safer. Allie knew from experience that even when the angels were posing as humans, they could instantly switch to their angelic form when necessary.

"How about You send the boys and have them create a diversion and I can go in and get Nick out."

Zad snorted and they looked at him. "You told me he was shackled. Most likely the 'new and improved' demon created shackles. How do you think you're going to get him out?"

Dang it... she hadn't thought about that. "Um, okay, how about you get Nick out and fly off with him while Duward and I create a diversion, and then as soon as you're outta there, I'll transfer Duward out."

Zad rolled his eyes. "And how do you think you're going to get into the army camp without being recognized? There aren't exactly women there you know."

"So, I dress like a soldier. Cut my hair off. Whatever. There're so many people in the camps that no one is going to pay attention to me."

Abba made a "hmm" sound. "While I'd rather you stay behind, I think your idea does hold merit," He said, and a wave of relief ran over Allie. "I know that you won't rest until your husband is safe and that you won't be able to concentrate on anything else, little warrior," He smiled softly and patted her hand.

Allie's eyes instantly filled at the memory of Metatron's nickname for her. Abba shook his head, his white hair flowing around his shoulders.

"No, no, none of that. I already told you he's just resting. At peace. And besides, there's no crying in wartime."

Allie laughed and then leaned over to hug her Savior again. As His arms wrapped around her, she felt something strange happen to her body. She released Him and looked down.

She was wearing a new uniform.

On the surface, it looked like one of Lucifer's soldier's uniforms, but she could tell it was no ordinary fabric, but seemed to be made from the same material that her other uniform had been made from.

Her arms felt a bit heavy too, so she pulled the cuff back and stared at the wide gold bracelets that had appeared on her wrists.

"My shackles," Abba told her with a wink. "Now the demons won't be able to put theirs on you."

"Awesome," Allie breathed. It would be such a relief to not have to worry about that again.

Abba stood. "Now, get going you two. And hurry back. You have a war to prepare for."

Chapter 19

RESCUING NICK WAS a breeze, compared to all the other things they'd had to do in recent memory. Once they transferred to Duward and the others and Allie had explained what they were going to do, they transferred to the outside of the camp at one of their previous safe bases.

Zad transformed into a frail, freckle-faced man that was so different from his angelic appearance that Allie had laughed hard. Even Duward laughed. Zad used his Old Age hand gesture on them, which made them both laugh even more.

"That reminds me," Allie told Duward as she helped him put on the uniform Zad had swiped from one of the outskirt tents, "how is it you know so much about the Old Age? I mean, you seem to get my references to old movies even. No one ever understands me."

Duward smiled at her as he pulled on the jacket that was far too tight for his abundant muscles. "I lived in the Old Age."

Allie's eyes almost bugged out; as far as she knew, everyone who'd come through the Tribulation without taking the mark of the beast had moved to The City or the Gardens.

Duward seemed to understand her confusion. He

shrugged. "My father was a miner," he reminded her. "He wanted to continue doing that, so we stayed in Kidal."

"So, you weren't believers when you survived the Tribulation?" She already knew the answer to that, because Abba had said Duward *would be* one of His children, not that he already was.

He shook his head as he pulled on the boots that looked far too small. "No, but my mama knew that we shouldn't take the mark. She didn't say how she knew, but just called it an 'evil eye' and 'Satan's spot'."

Duward straightened then and Zad put his hand on the man's shoulder, which was kind of funny because in his new human form he had to reach up to do so.

"And now? Are you a believer? Are you going to trust Abba, to know that He is the only Way to eternal life?"

Duward nodded eagerly. "Oh yeah, I already decided that not long after I found Alejandro in the cell. Even bloody and beat up, he was witnessing to me," he laughed. "I had to work things out in my head, but I knew that Abba is the only choice for me."

Allie whooped and hugged her huge friend. "Thank Abba! Glad to call you brother now," she grinned up at him, then cocked her head toward the army.

"Okay, let's go make a scene."

~~

Allie wasn't sure which tent she'd seen Nick in and of course there was the possibility that he'd been moved, so she moved into the spirit again and sought him out.

Thankfully, her husband hadn't been further injured in the hours they'd been gone. In fact, he seemed to sense her presence and she waited for him to join her.

"Hey," he smiled.

"Hey yourself," Allie smiled back. *"Came to get you outta here. It's gonna be Zad, but he looks like a strawberry farmer, just so you know."*

Nick laughed, the swirls of color that surrounded him twirling in a wispy dance. *"Okay. Glad to know you didn't get captured. For once."*

She smirked. *"Smart alec. For that, I should just leave you here."* She made a move like she was kissing him, but of course there was no substance to the form.

"See ya soon." Allie then moved outside the tent and used her newfound "flying" skill to rise above the area so she could get a grip of where it was.

Of course, right next to Lucifer's camp.

She moved back to her body and told the others, so they transferred to an area behind some boulders directly across from the tent where Nick was being held.

"Okay, so it's fifty-seven tents to the east," she told the others. "I suggest you let me transfer you to a place I saw between tents and then we'll get Operation Sic Nick underway."

"Seriously?" Zad drawled while Duward laughed.

"What?" Allie said with mock seriousness. "You don't like that? How 'bout Operation Pick Nick? No? Dang, tough crowd," she muttered, then she grabbed the guys' shoulders and transferred them.

"What are we going to do for a diversion?" Duward muttered as they walked toward the tent grouping adjacent to where Nick was being held. It was on the opposite side of Lucifer's camp, but still way too close for Allie's comfort.

"Crud, I hadn't thought of that," Allie grumbled. They passed some other soldiers and Allie nodded her head in greeting, careful to keep the shadow from the brim of her hat on her face. The soldiers would flip if they knew a female was in the midst.

"Got it," she told Duward. "You yank my hat off, yell 'It's a woman!' or something, then grab me like you've captured me. That should make enough of a scene for Zad to get in and grab Nick."

Her friend looked at her like she was insane. "What? It's a good plan!" she argued in a hiss. Duward shook his head but sighed in defeat.

"Yell loud," she told him, "so we get as many

soldiers running over here as possible."

The plan worked surprisingly well. The only problem came when they met back at the base and remembered that they couldn't transfer Nick with the shackles.

"Dang it, forgot about that," Allie muttered. Not only could they not transfer him, they didn't even have a contrans to travel in.

"Guess I'll just have to fly him," Zad sighed. He looked at Nick. "We're gonna have to get pretty high to be out of firing range. Hope you're not prone to nose bleeds," he said as he grabbed the guy, tossed him on his back and took to the sky.

"No, he just gets airsick!" Allie joked as they flew off. She laughed when she heard Zad moan.

~~

The remaining residents of the Gardens — the farmers who didn't want to leave their crops unharvested — were moved into The City, and the Remnants and angels worked to set up a perimeter around The City.

Nick plotted and planned for every possible contingency, while Allie tried to make sure all the soldiers had what they needed and were clear on the plans. The angels worked to ensure the humans were trained in fighting. As much as they could do in a few weeks anyway.

By the time the dust cloud from the approaching

invasion could be seen on the far horizon, Allie was thankful that Abba was going to win the war, because there was no way the ragtag group they had was ready for what was coming.

In just days, the army reached the outskirts of the Gardens and proceeded to surround it. The defenders watched as more soldiers than could be counted marched around the perimeter. It reminded Allie of the old story of Jericho.

Only this time, the bad guys were marching around the city.

"They'll attack in two days," Abba said as they stood on top of The City wall.

Allie turned to Him. "That soon?" Even though she knew that the good guys were going to win this battle, her heart still leapt a bit in fear. The army was incredibly huge... and those on Abba's side were far outnumbered.

"At dawn two days from now they'll start their offense. First, they'll work on pushing through the line in the Gardens. Then, after they succeed in that, they'll try to break through The City walls." He looked at her, His multicolored eyes sparkling, when Allie thought they should be troubled.

"They won't breach the walls. They'll be defeated before then."

Allie turned her gaze back to the troops stomping dust clouds into the air. "Why not just take them out now? Why let them get their evil feet in the

Gardens?"

Abba smirked at her. "It's not their feet that are evil; it's their hearts, silly girl." He sighed then and stared out at the multitude with her.

"The reason I will let this go on is because even at the last hour, others will decide to trust in Me. It isn't until the very last one of My children finally returns home that I will judge creation."

Allie never liked to think too hard on Judgment Day. It was scary, even for one who had already chosen to follow Abba.

His hand slid to her shoulder, immediately providing comfort. "All will be right, daughter. You just have to do your part."

Allie sighed. "I will." She laughed then and held out her arms where the gold cuffs still encircled her wrists. "And I'm not taking these puppies off until this is all over. Not going back to Loserfer again."

Abba threw back His head and laughed. "Oh, My dear child, eternity is going to be so much fun with you there."

They left the wall and walked back down into The City. Usually a bustling, happy place filled with citizens who all knew one another and greeted each other with a friendly kiss, the atmosphere was now subdued. Anxious.

"I guess I should get back to the troops," Allie said reluctantly. She was feeling a bit unneeded, what with Nick handling the planning and the angels doing all the training. There wasn't a whole lot for her to do.

"You're needed to boost morale," Abba told her as He reached for her hand, pulling it up and patting it with His other. "Just seeing the Mistress will encourage the others to stand strong."

Allie nodded and glanced down. Abba had given her yet another new uniform, this one even shinier and more ornate than the one she'd worn for her journey through Lucifer's army.

"Well, at least they're going to be able to see me coming," she drawled. Abba laughed.

"That was the idea."

Chapter 20

THE TROOPS WERE as ready as they were ever going to be, Allie finally decided. Over and over again, though, she was forced to remind herself that the battle might be theirs, and they might even lose — which was looking more and more likely, just from the sheer numbers they were facing — but the war belonged to Abba.

And the victory.

Nick had decided to break off Abba's army into smaller battalions, each led by a Remnant. He was hoping to protect The City from all sides and while Allie hated leaving her husband's side again, it was necessary.

She led her group of soldiers to the east, toward the farmlands of the Gardens. Her battalion was the largest, because they had the most ground to cover.

Once the group was positioned, Allie climbed on top of a boulder so they could see her. The sun was just beginning to set, it's coppery golden light reflecting off her armor, almost blindingly. She pointed her sword to the sky to draw everyone's attention.

"In just a short time, we will be facing the enemy," she yelled. "They outnumber us four to one and are better armed. From a military standpoint, the odds are not in our favor."

There was shuffling as the troops absorbed the uncomfortable news. Allie knew most of them grasped the knowledge that they were outnumbered, and it was a near impossibility that they were going to win. Or even survive.

She grinned then, even though most of the faces staring at her wore grim expressions.

"Many of us will die today. Maybe even most of us. But now that you've chosen the right side, Abba's side, that death will mean nothing, because soon we will all be living forever!" There was cheering at that and Allie's grin widened.

"Fight with everything you have in you. Don't back down," she said, emphasizing each word. "Most of all, fight the good fight, show no fear, you have *nothing* to fear! Welcome death, should it come, laughing in its face, because even death has no hold on you!" She paused, letting the troops absorb that.

With a deep breath, she then bellowed, "Abba *promises* He will win this war!"

Another wide grin crossed her face then; Allie was sure that the cheers from the troops were loud enough to reach Lucifer's ears.

She could swear she heard him cursing.

~~

The attack came swiftly and savagely.

While Abba's people fought like they had nothing to fear, Lucifer's army fought as though they had nothing to lose, and that made for a very ferocious enemy.

Allie summoned all the anger and frustration she'd felt while being held captive in Lucifer's grip. She chopped through soldier after soldier, not sparing any much of a glance. She didn't like hurting people, not even those who wanted her dead, so she had to keep her focus on the fact that they were protecting Abba's people. Protecting The City.

Abba had given orders to "incapacitate, but not kill." Allie knew He was wanting to give the people every chance to accept Him, up to the very last minute. That was just His way. While she, as a human, never quite grasped His unending patience and mercy, she was in awe of it nonetheless.

Even the angels, while fighting physically, fought even harder spiritually. The entire Heavenly Host had taken to the air and it was truly amazing to watch as they soared above, slashing and hacking at humans and demons alike. Before each kill, though, they would bellow:

"Choose the Lion and live forever! Follow the beast and die!"

In their last moment of life on the earth, many more chose to live.

Fighting bravely, Abba's troops held the enemy back for much longer than Allie thought they could. She was proud of her fellow warriors as they fought fiercely, cutting through the line as it surged forward.

Lucifer's troops seemed to be surprised by the intensity with which Abba's people fought.

The fight continued for what seemed like days, but Allie knew it was probably only hours. Despite the long practices every day, she and the Remnants wearied. Practice wasn't quite the same as trying to survive.

Allie continued hacking and slashing, begging the fallen to accept Abba until her throat was raw. She was exhausted. Her arm was aching, her shoulders burned and her chest heaved from exertion. She was at the point of dropping her sword and letting the next demon or human take her head off. But then she saw something that reenergized her and brought her focus back to the fight.

Lucifer.

He wasn't fighting, just strolling among his line of warriors with a maniacal grin on his face. A face that was far too beautiful to belong to one so hideous. Allie's lip curled up. Abba didn't allow His children to hate, but if there was one who deserved to be despised, it was the original fallen angel.

She hacked at several more soldiers, stepping over their writhing bodies, intent on getting closer to the beast who had threatened to wear her head as a helmet during this battle. She smirked; he was too late for that.

"Hey, Loserfer," she yelled, using her new favorite nickname for the jerk, "you do know you're losing this war, right? Abba wins and you and any who don't change to the good side are gonna burn forever. That's a long time, huh?"

She didn't miss the way some of the soldiers stiffened at her comment. They'd heard the same thing from Alejandro, but maybe now it was finally sinking in.

Allie watched as the fallen angel turned to her, his beautiful face morphing into a mask of rage. *Dang, he really hates me,* she thought with a grin, glad that he did. Meant she had done her job well.

Lucifer marched toward her, shoving aside his own soldiers who were battling against Remnants and those on Abba's side. Allie, in turn, brought down two more soldiers as she made her way to him.

This time, their meeting was going to be on her terms.

She was a few arms' lengths away from him now and her sword arm suddenly felt rejuvenated as a surge of energy moved through her.

"Remember the last time we were together? When I kicked you in your itty bitty marbles and brought you to your knees?" she taunted. "This time, I think I'll cut those marbles off and feed them to my bobcat."

The angel of darkness growled at that and shoved the last soldier in his way to the side as he stomped up to her. Allie was ready, though and surged forward and stabbed the sword Abba Himself had made for her right through the devil's heart.

Of course, he didn't die. That would have been nice, she thought, but better still that he would burn forever for his innumerable crimes. He, and all the other angels who'd chosen to follow him, were the only beings who didn't deserve Abba's forgiveness.

Allie could see the pain in the creature's eyes, even though he didn't say anything as he stepped back, forcing the sword from his body. She thought about following to keep the sword implanted in him, but she didn't. Better to pull it out and hit him somewhere else.

Like the neck.

She brought her sword back to take his head off as she wondered what would happen if she *did* manage to cut off the serpent's head. *Since he won't die, would he carry his head around until Judgment?* She giggled at the thought as she swung.

Just as Allie started to swing, she felt a *whoosh* and felt the brush of wings against her face. She stopped her swing just in time to keep from slicing Zad's wings off as he swooped in between her and Lucifer.

Probably thought he was protecting her. Allie rolled her eyes, disappointed that she wouldn't get the chance to see Lucifer walking around holding his head like a helmet.

"You aren't getting near her again," Zad growled, his massive beating wings causing the air to brush against her cheeks, drying the sweat that had accumulated.

Lucifer laughed, but it was a bitter sound. "Zadkiel, Abba's messenger boy… what? Now you're Alessandra's bodyguard?"

Zad didn't respond, but he took a step back, closer to Allie. His wings curled toward her, creating walls on both sides. *He's protecting me?* She wanted to yell at him for the insult, but at the same time, she was touched.

"Get back to your minions, Abaddon," Zad drawled. "You have a war to lose."

"Oooohhhh," Allie called out, "that's gotta hurt."

Lucifer said something that Allie couldn't hear. She realized Zad's wings must have been sort of sound proofing, which ticked her off. She wanted to hear what the enemy was saying, but she also wanted him to hear her taunts.

It was her last chance to give him a hard time, after all.

She reached up and poked Zad in the sides. He flinched, but didn't move the wings, so she did it again, harder this time. He squirmed, then finally moved the wings back to the sides. Allie stepped around him in time to see Lucifer storming off. She whacked Zad in the arm with the back of his arm.

"Party pooper," she grumbled while he laughed.

"Come on," he said, "we have a war to get back to."

The taunting from Zad and Allie must have

revitalized Lucifer, as he went back to his troops and called his leaders to gather around him. Allie watched as they seemed to be listening intently, then all ran off in different directions to their own platoons.

The army suddenly rallied, finding a source of energy for one last push from whatever it was Lucifer told them. *Lies, of course,* Allie thought. But whatever he'd said, it was effective.

Before she could make it back to her own battalion and warn them, the enemy surged forward, fighting with new vigor. Though they fought valiantly, the Remnants and the new believer soldiers were forced back, into The City.

And just as on that day, the last day of the Tribulation, a loud trumpet sounded, stopping everyone in their tracks as every eye looked to the heavens. Throughout the millennia, trumpets had been used to announce great events, to herald both good and bad. In this case, it was both.

Allie knew the time had come.

Abba was going to seal the fate of the damned.

Epilogue

COLOR. SO MUCH COLOR. Not only shades, but waves. Vibrations. Specks. Glow.

And the sound. Whispers, tremors, pings, tones, chimes. The ghostly breath of a miniscule insect, so insignificant that even the most perceptive ears wouldn't have heard it.

The air... tasted. The enchanting smell in the air was one thing, but the flavor of the atmosphere was intoxicating.

"Daughter..." His voice was as soothing as the gentlest touch, the softest stroke.

She turned toward the voice, a smile on her face. "Abba," she whispered, because speaking wasn't really necessary. She could hear His thoughts, and He, hers.

"What do you think?" His hand swept over the area and her eyes followed.

What do I think? There were no words. It was... indescribable.

The scene before them was unlike anything she'd ever seen, but she knew it was unlike anything ever seen before. What was before them was a brand-new creation. And she knew it was made for her.

But not just for her. There were countless others here, moving about in a deep state of awe like she;

the feelings that couldn't be described with mere words surrounding them in brilliant, wavy auras. She laughed then; she could actually *see* others' feelings.

As far as the eye could see, beauty. Wonder. Glory. It was as if Abba took all that made Him incredible and created an entire world with it.

At their feet were rolling hills with every manner of flora and fauna, so colorful that it almost hurt to look at. Buzzing insects that she knew would no longer cause harm unlocked the fragrance from the blossoms as they danced among the buds.

The scent that tickled her senses was intoxicating. It seemed to seep deep into her pores, although she didn't think she had such things any longer. She wasn't sure she even had skin, although the others seemed to.

Beyond the hills in the distance stood majestic mountains, painted deep magenta and lavender. Brilliant white snow topped the peaks, so white that she knew no impurities were to be found in this incredible place. It was fresh, new, pure.

Unlike in the old place, there was a great body of water — *a sea*, she remembered such a thing being called — afar off. Huge creatures could be seen gliding on the surface, then diving, leaping out of the glistening turquoise water that sparkled like gems. They were playing, joyous in their new home.

Emerald forests with trees so tall they seemed to reach all the way to the stars dotted the landscape in massive groupings, separating the other areas. She could see all manner of creatures in the thick forests, some scooting up into the tall branches, others dancing around in the lush grass below, and the feathered ones soaring from treetop to treetop.

She turned then to survey the place where she stood with the Creator. A palace, unlike anything mere man could have created, more glorious than even Solomon's temple, sparkled and shimmered before them.

Created from all the precious gems ever known — and likely many that were never discovered by man — the massive building caught each glimmer of the light and twinkled. It was mesmerizing.

She knew that the light came from Abba. There was no longer a sun or moon, nor any need for either. He was the only light, the only warmth, they needed. He was   and always had been — *all* any creature ever required.

Now that they were changed, perfected, He was in His full glory. So bright, so brilliant, no creature could have ever looked upon Him before and survived.

But now — He was even more glorious than ever.

They were standing on a tower with the palace grounds stretching before them, sprawling with even more vegetation than was seen outside the palace grounds. While it seemed to be perfectly manicured, she knew the plants were left to grow as they would. But they grew to please Abba, who like order.

Abba had asked a question, but she didn't know how to answer. There were no words to describe how she felt about all she had seen. But even more than the magnificent splendor surrounding them, the love that filled her was nearly overwhelming. Bursting from her like a geyser, it caught the fragrant breeze and floated over the landscape, wrapping all the new world in a cocoon of adoration.

And it was all coming from the Creator.

She tried to compare the new world with the old, but strangely, she had very little memory of what was before. Even her old name was gone, but she knew she didn't need it now. Abba had given her a new one, so beautiful that she thought she should cry each time she heard it. But there were no tears in this place.

She knew there were relationships she'd had before, but they were gone too. In their place was a love affair with every human in the new world. They were all brothers and sisters, brethren.

But they were more. So much more.

The shimmering palace, the gently rolling hills, the aromatic flowers, the towering trees, the azure sky, the adorable creatures, the majestic mountains — while incredibly amazing and shockingly beautiful, they were nothing compared to the love.

Finally, she turned back to the Creator and gazed into His glowing face which radiated the feelings she had back to her. She smiled, knowing He knew exactly what she thought.

"Wow."

Beloved:

Thank you for reading!

I know that many are asking, "What about Judgment Day? Why did you skip over that?" Well, honestly, throughout the series I only wished to convey Abba's great patience, mercy and most of all, love.

As believers, we know that Day will be terrifying for those who have refused Abba. I wonder, though, if it will be just as frightening for those of us who have accepted the Lord. The difference is that we *know* where we'll end up, that despite the fact we deserve the same punishment as those who refused the Lord's forgiveness, we'll live with Him forever!

That is what I chose to focus on, not the horrors of that Day.

I hope you liked this series, but even more, I hope that through my writing efforts you have grasped the fact that the Father loves you so very much and that He wants what is best for you. The only thing He has ever wanted is our love and for us to love others.

Think of how much we could change the world if we would just love!

Speaking of... I love you!

VJJ Dunn

Check out VJJ's other books!

Beginning the End, Book 1 of The End Series

My name is Nikki. Just a country gal with no real mad skills. But after the global economic collapse, my husband Reg and I found ourselves leading a ragtag group of survivors, those who managed to escape the cities...and the Neos. The Neo Geo Task Force is the new government. The new world order. They were supposed to be the law of the land, the peacekeepers. They were anything but.

Surviving the End, Book 2 of The End Series

This time, our present, was the end of the age. Or, at least the slippery downward slope heading toward the end. My name is Nikki and with my husband Reg we tried our best to protect our growing group of survivors. Everything that happened had been foretold in ancient texts, some written long before Christ walked the earth. But even knowing the prophesy didn't completely prepare us for just how difficult those times would be.

Embracing the End, Book 3 of The End Series

While the rest of the world was celebrating the establishment of the "new world order," we were struggling just to eat. We fought to live, to exist. We never could have imagined just how bad things would get. But betrayal was our worst enemy. The Lord never left us, though. His promises kept us going, gave us direction. He led us and guided our steps, even when those steps took us right up to the Neos' doorstep. And then we were no longer fighting. We were storming the gates of Hell.

Conquering the End Book 4 of The End Series

The hunt continues. But now the entire world is after us. We are Followers of The Way—believers of the Christ. Our enemy, the Neos, have morphed into something even worse than the demon-possessed Satan minions they were. Now they rule the world and their quest is to annihilate anyone who stands in their way. Which means us. We know that Christ wins in the end; we just have to survive until then. We just hope the last day comes quickly, because the earth is going to Hell.

Mama's Heart, Book 1 in The Tapestry Series

Misty is shocked to learn she's pregnant, and out of wedlock too. But all things work out, until a fateful day when her entire world is turned upside down. Misty becomes bitter, angry, and questions everything she ever knew about God. But a surprise visit from a stranger helps her put life into perspective and to see God's handiwork in weaving the tapestry of her life.

Unanswered Prayers, Book 2 in The Tapestry Series

Steve Tyler is the typical mid-western kid...a little nerdy, very smart, with a great future. Through a series of life-changing events and "unanswered" prayers, Steve turns his back on God and turns to drugs for his comfort. Homeless, friendless and hopeless where every day is a struggle just to survive, Steve finds himself in such a deep valley that the only way up is by taking God's hand.

Here, Hold My Beer, Confessions of the Common Sense Challenged Male

Stories that will break your funny bone and keep you in stitches...and you won't have to go to the ER! Humor satire about the dumb things that guys will sometimes do. You know, those decisions that usually start with a trip to the liquor store and end up with a trip to the hospital. If you like to hear those "chill around the fire pit, guzzling six packs and spitting tobacco at the flames" kind of stories, this book is for you!

Find and follow VJJ Dunn on:

Amazon (VJJ Dunn)

Facebook ("AuthorVJJDunn")

Instagram ("@authorvjjdunn")

Pinterest ("Author VJJ Dunn")

Twitter ("@AuthorVJJDunn")

Website www.vjjdunn.com

Printed in Great Britain
by Amazon